THE ROOT OF ALL EVIL

GLOCK GRANNIES COZY MYSTERY, BOOK 2

SHANNON VANBERGEN

FAIRFIELD PUBLISHING

DEDICATION

*A special thank you to my sister Wendi Dunham
for bringing Les to life with her poems. She's not just my
sister, she's also one of my closest friends.*

CHAPTER 1

BRAN MUFFINS AND STRONG COFFEE—TWO THINGS THAT get you going in more ways than one. At least that was what the Grannies told me. And judging by the amount of both sitting on the counter, they must have been on their way over.

"Oh," I said excitedly. "Are we having a meeting today?"

Grandma Dean looked my way and gave me a once-over, following it up with a disappointing shake of her head. Grandma Dean was always impeccably dressed… I was not.

She carried the muffins to the table. "*We* do not have a meeting. *I* have a meeting."

"But I'm part of the group," I protested. I pulled some butter from the fridge to remind her how useful I was. "You made me a member and I even helped solve a murder!"

Grandma took the butter and put it next to the muffins. "Think of yourself as an understudy," she said, walking to the drawer to pull out a butter knife.

Grandma Dean used to be a famous actor, dancer, and singer in Europe back in the day. She still carried herself like an old movie star and liked to make theater references.

"But even an understudy has to know the part!"

"Your part is silent." Grandma flashed me a look that told me I wasn't going to win this argument. Then her face softened.

"I don't want you to get too caught up in our...card club..."

"You don't have to keep calling it that. I know what you do!" I had found out a few weeks ago that Grandma's "card club" was really a neighborhood watch on steroids...and maybe Ensure. They didn't just "watch" the neighborhood, they protected it...with force. They called themselves the Glock Grannies.

"Well, whatever I want to call it, it's too dangerous for you. If we need your help again, we'll let you know."

I wanted to protest further, but knew it was futile.

"Why don't you go down to the shop and start setting things up? The back is full of inventory that just came in yesterday." I sighed, and Grandma Dean reached up to smooth my hair. "Don't look so disappointed. This meeting is going to be boring. We have so much to do downtown and it would be great if you got a head start."

I finally agreed and walked toward my room, grabbing a bran muffin on the way.

"And Nikki," she called after me. I turned to look at her. "Do something about that hair. People are going to think something lives in there."

You wouldn't know it by the way she talked to me about my hair and lack of fashion sense, but she loved me fiercely. That was a good a way to describe Geraldine Dean—fierce. She was also kind and loyal, but she did everything with a ferocity and tenacity that seemed to leave everyone else in the dust.

"You've got ten minutes," Grandma hollered from the kitchen.

I sighed and looked at myself in the mirror. I really was a mess. I had come to stay with Grandma Dean nearly two months ago at the urging of my mother. She said I needed to leave our small Illinois farm town to get some clarity after a string of marriages and divorces—six to be exact. Apparently, the whole family thought I married out of boredom and when guy number seven put a ring on my finger, it was finally time to break the cycle.

Bo was number seven, or he would be if I married him. He was different than the others, though…he was real. And that terrified me, which was why I had agreed to come stay with Grandma Dean.

I looked down at the few hair products that lined my bathroom sink and then glanced back up at myself. I was going to need something heavy duty to tame this mess. I quickly got dressed and ran to Grandma Dean's bathroom. She had every hair and makeup product the world had to offer. I opened a closet that was nothing but bottle after bottle of elixirs and was suddenly overwhelmed.

"Grandma Dean," I called to her. "What should I do if I want to tame my hair a bit today?"

I could hear her coming so I stepped back from the closet. She walked in and looked at me with a face full of pity. "Go back in time and convince your mother not to marry your father. She has the most beautiful hair and she married that man even though she had to know his genes were condemning all her children and grandchildren to this." She waved her arms wildly in the air, encircling me.

"If I did that," I reminded her, "then I wouldn't exist."

"And then you wouldn't have a problem with your hair now, would you?" She laughed at her joke and gave me a hug. "I only have a minute but I'll do the best I can." She hollered for Kitty Purry, one of her cats named after celebrities. The other was Catalie Portman. Kitty was the one she consulted on any kind of fashion emergency. Catalie was more laid back and preferred less attention. Kitty was Grandma's favorite; Catalie was mine.

After being called, Kitty Purry came bouncing in wearing a red sparkling tutu with a white shirt that had a rhinestone heart in the middle. The cat dressed better than I did.

I sat on a stool in front of Grandma Dean's makeup table and Grandma Dean went to work. She spritzed and sprayed and smoothed, while telling me for the hundredth time that if I would just do this or that straight out of the shower, I could avoid this mess.

When she was done, she stood back to look at her piece of art. "What do you think, Kitty Purry?" she asked the cat, who was sitting on the table and staring at me intently. Kitty meowed and Grandma sprung up. "Oh my goodness!" She pulled open a drawer. "Thank you for reminding me!" She bent down and kissed Kitty on the head. She handed me some lip gloss. "Here," she said, putting it in my hands and folding my fingers over it like she was handing down a family heirloom I should protect with my life. "You'll need this."

Before she could say any more, there was a knock at the door. "Put that on and get out of here," she said as she disappeared through the door. "We'll have dinner tonight, anywhere you like…as long as it's not fast food."

I stared at myself in the mirror as I heard the first of the Grannies arrive, their high-pitched chatter in the kitchen quickly going from grandkids to bowel movements.

Grandma Dean was a miracle worker—my curls were about as tame as they were ever going to get and they smelled like a French garden. I looked at the lip gloss. For a moment, I thought about slipping it back in her drawer, but I knew she would stop me on the way out and make me put it on. I slid the tube across my lips and a glossy pink flowed over them. It really was amazing what a little lip gloss could do.

As I walked through the kitchen and toward the door, the Grannies gave me a strange look. "Don't worry," Grandma Dean said to them as she handed me the keys to her car. "She's heading to the shop." She smiled at me and then a chorus of "good-byes" rang out from the Grannies.

As I walked down the sidewalk of the retirement community and toward the parking lot to Grandma Dean's car, I couldn't help but think how unfair this was. I should be in there with them! I even went through a sort of initiation! After I refused to take a blood oath of secrecy, they decided I could join their little group if I got my eyebrows done. I had agreed and, after sitting in the mall going through something called "threading," I wished I had just taken the blood oath. My eyebrows came out great, though, so I couldn't complain about it too much. But here I was, after going through all of that, and I was still being banished from one of their meetings.

What could they be talking about in there? I wondered.

My curiosity was piqued when two older gentlemen passed me on the sidewalk just before I got to Grandma's car. I turned and watched them walk up to Grandma Dean's door. The tall one smiled at me when he passed; he looked tired and stressed out. The other man, who was shorter, completely ignored me and grumbled something as he stormed ahead.

I saw Grandma open the door for them, a serious look on her face. She glanced around to see who might be watching and caught me staring. She forced a smile and waved, before closing the door.

What was going on in there? As much as I wanted to know, I knew the Glock Grannies didn't miss anything and I would be caught if I tried snooping. It was better to just go on with my day and hope that Grandma Dean confided in me later.

CHAPTER 2

I STOOD THERE IN OUR NEW SHOP DOWNTOWN, *Hello, Beautiful Boutique,* and started to go through the boxes of new arrivals. It had taken Grandma Dean and I several days to decide on a name. It was hard to come up with a name for a shop that contained clothing for both women and cats, especially one that wasn't vulgar. We finally settled on *Hello, Beautiful* when Grandma said she just wanted people to feel beautiful. We decided to shout that out every time a customer walked in the door. I'm a little more of an introvert than Grandma Dean, but it still seemed like a greeting I could manage.

I opened a box and pulled out a handful of fleece cat sweatshirts in various colors. As I hung them, I couldn't help but look around the little store with pride. Just a few weeks ago, this place had been completely gutted thanks to a fire. Before the fire, it was an antique store, *Junk in the Trunk*, that Grandma Dean had owned and ran. But after someone set it on fire to hide a dirty secret, Grandma moved her shop down the street. Now that she had the keys back to this place and it was all cleaned up, Grandma Dean and I decided to go into business together. The human clothes were my idea; the cat clothes were hers.

"Need some help?" A booming voice scared me and I spun around to see where it came from. Joe Delluci, AKA the Hunky Fireman, stood at the front of the store. His big sparking smile made my stomach flip.

"Sure," I said, nodding toward some boxes. "Wanna open those for me?"

Joe grabbed the box cutter from the floor next to a stack of boxes. I couldn't help but notice the muscles in his arm bulge as he sliced the first box open. "What in the heck is this?" He pulled out a tiny cat tutu.

"Cat clothes," I said over my shoulder as I hung up the last sweatshirt, this one with the word "Love" bejeweled across the back. "And not just any cat clothes, but designer cat clothes, if you can imagine it."

He laughed. "Leave it to Geraldine."

We worked silently for a few minutes and I tried not to stare at him. He was a gorgeous piece of work. His Italian heritage was obvious with his dark skin, hair, and eyes. He perfectly filled out his tight jeans and black t-shirt and I couldn't help but notice how his sleeves fell at the middle of his biceps, showing off a giant bulge of muscle. Oh, how I'd like to swing from those.

"Nikki…"

Hearing my name snapped me back to reality.

"Were you even listening to me?"

Crap. "Uh, sorry…I just have a lot on my mind trying to organize the store before we open next week." I held my breath to see if he bought it.

He smiled and ran a hand through his thick hair. "Maybe you need a break from all this. Want to meet for coffee later? Maybe at the *Palm Breeze*?"

I loved the *Palm Breeze*. It was a trendy coffee shop that looked more like a snow cone hut with its bright blue and white exterior and beach-themed interior. They had the best coconut frappes there… Well, I assumed they were the best. I hadn't actually had a coconut frappe from anywhere else.

"I would love to." I smiled, trying not to seem too eager, even though I was.

"Great! Meet me there about three?"

I agreed and non-apologetically watched his butt as he walked out of the store. When he was gone, I sighed heavily. I was doing it again! Why couldn't I keep my mind off men? Then again, how could I with someone like Joe in the room? He was the kind of guy who would walk down the street and the whole world would stop and stare. Not only was he hot, he had the perfect smile and sparkling personality to round him out.

I got back to work and hummed as I went. This day was turning out nicely after all.

Suddenly, I got this strange feeling like someone was watching me. I cautiously looked around and sure enough, there was a man, maybe late twenties or possibly early thirties like myself, standing outside and looking in through the large shop windows. As soon as he saw me, his face went red. He stuffed his hands in his pockets and quickly spun to the right, walking away.

Who was that? How long had he been standing there? Suddenly, I wished the shop had curtains that I could close like Grandma's antique shop down the street. I decided to see where the man had gone and quickly made my way to the front of the store, leaping over boxes as I went.

I opened the door and looked toward where he had run off. He hadn't made it very far. He was waiting to cross the busy street and just before he crossed, he turned around and looked my way. He nervously took off across the street, tripping and nearly falling halfway. I watched him as he safely made it to the other side and then ducked into a record store. Strange. I stood there for a little while, waiting to see if he would come out again, but after several minutes, I gave up and went back to work.

I kept busy the rest of the day, hanging up clothes and tagging them. To my surprise, I worked right though lunch. But by the time 2:30 rolled around, I was starving. I decided to head over to the coffee shop a few minutes early and maybe grab a bagel or two before Joe got there. Other than when he kissed me about a month earlier, we had managed to stay just friends, but that didn't mean I didn't try to keep my carb obsession from him.

A few minutes later, I was pulling into the coffee shop and I immediately saw two older men walking though the parking lot and up to the building. *I recognize those guys*, I thought. I watched as they stopped for a moment, the shorter one taking a minute to yell something at a couple of young guys walking past them. "And pull up your pants!" I heard him yell after them. Even from my distance, I could see the taller man's face go red in embarrassment.

Suddenly, the sound of screeching tires filled the parking lot. Before I even had a chance to glance around to see where it was coming from, a white car sped through the lot right toward the two old guys. I screamed "watch out!" from the car, even though there was no way they could hear me. To my surprise, the old men were quick and agile. They managed to narrowly escape the oncoming car by leaping between two parked vehicles. The white car turned sharply and avoided hitting the row of parked cars, speeding away just as quickly as it had arrived.

I flew out of my car and to the men who were crouched on the ground between the cars. "Are you okay?" I asked them, out of breath.

"Is he gone?" the tall one asked me.

I glanced around to double-check, then assured him he was. I held out my hand and pulled him up. I reached out to help his friend, but he smacked it away. "I can get up myself," he grumbled.

I gave them a quick look up and down. "Are you guys okay?"

The taller man was shaking and I put my arm out for him to grab on to. The shorter one started to yell at others who were coming up and asking if they were all right. "There's nothing to see here. You people just mind your own darn business!"

"They're just concerned," I said, sticking up for the people he was shooing away. "You were almost run over!"

"Oh really?" he barked. "I thought Stan and I were just crouched down here playing a quick game of Twister!"

Was it bad to wish someone had been a victim of vehicular homicide?

Before long, a string of police cars were pulling into the parking lot. The taller man still hadn't let go of my arm so I stood there next to him, reassuring him everything would be okay. Detective Owen Russell got out of his car and made his way over to us. I had a bit of history with Detective Russell. After Grandma Dean's shop burned down, he asked me out for coffee. My boy-crazy mind thought it was a date, but it turned out to be him just trying to get some info on my Grandmother, who was his number one suspect. It was an innocent mistake, one I promised myself I'd never make again...yet knew I most likely would.

"Nikki," he said, surprised to see me. "Are you okay?"

"Nothing is wrong with her," the short, old man snapped. "We're the ones who were nearly killed. What's it take to get a statement taken around here? Apparently, boobs and a bad haircut!"

My face went red. I didn't know who that short man was, but I was about ready to run him over myself.

"Mr. Henson," Detective Owen said calmly. "Would you like to tell me what happened?"

The old man grumbled something under his breath then answered. "It's the same as last time! Someone tried to kill me! How many attempts is it going to take before you finally decide to do something about it?"

Detective Owen put his hand out and grabbed the taller man's elbow. "You okay, Mr. Bennett?"

"Yah, just a little shook up is all. No worse for wear."

I felt bad for the taller man, Mr. Bennett. He seemed like a nice guy.

I finished giving my statement to Detective Owen just as Joe pulled in. As Joe made his way over, I saw Detective Owen glance at him and make a face. Was that jealousy I saw? Surely not.

Joe rushed to my side. "Nikki, are you all right?"

"Poodles is fine!" snapped the cranky Mr. Henson,

who was still standing behind Mr. Bennett and I. "What does it take to get some sympathy over here?"

I rolled my eyes and looked up at Mr. Bennett. "Are you going to be okay?"

"I'll make sure he's taken care of," Detective Owen said, pulling Mr. Bennett toward him a little. "You two go on. I'll make sure he gets home okay."

Mr. Bennett finally released my arm and I slowly walked away, feeling guilty for leaving him. I didn't even know the guy, but I could tell he was kind and I knew the ordeal had really shaken him up.

"What in the heck happened back there?" Joe asked as we walked into the coffee shop. I filled him in while we waited in line.

"The cranky one said it had happened before?"

I nodded as I looked into the display case that housed the baked goods. It all looked good, but I was too upset to eat. Just kidding. I was starving and the adrenaline rush made me feel ravenous. "I'll take a slice of blueberry pound cake and a bagel with brown sugar cream cheese...and let's throw in one of those palm tree shortbread cookies," I said to the man behind the counter.

I didn't even look over to see if Joe was judging me. My mind was on Mr. Henson and Mr. Bennett and their visit with Grandma Dean earlier. That was why they went to visit the Glock Grannies—because someone was trying to kill the cranky old Mr. Henson and they wanted the Grannies to figure out who was

15

behind it. *Well, maybe now that I know what's going on, and saw an attempted murder firsthand, they'll let me in*, I thought.

"Hey," I yelled to the man behind the counter as he started to walk away. "Give me one of those raisin biscuits too." I needed to keep up my strength. Carb loading before reloading…could that be my motto now that I was in the Glock Grannies group? I'd have to come up with something because I was pretty sure I was about to become an important part of their little club. Of course, if I had known just how important, I would've loaded up my pastries and left town instead of waltzing into Grandma Dean's apartment gloating because I had been at the scene of the crime. If I had only known what was in my future.

CHAPTER 3

I WALKED INTO GRANDMA DEAN'S APARTMENT AND found her straightening up the kitchen.

She smiled at me as she wiped down the counter. "How's the shop coming along?"

"Oh, just fine," I said nonchalantly.

"Great! You and I can head there in the morning and finish up whatever needs to be done. But for now, I'm going to read the newspaper and relax a bit."

As she walked out of the kitchen, I noticed she left the newspaper on the corner of the kitchen table.

"Grandma," I called after her. "You forgot your paper." I picked it up and held it out to her, but she only laughed.

"I read the news on my phone. Just throw it in the recycling bin."

I held the thin paper in my hand for a minute

before following her into the living room. "If you read it on your phone, then why do you get the paper?"

Grandma sighed like it was obvious. "Because by getting the paper, I'm supporting two local businesses —the newspaper and the recycling company."

I supposed she was right and sat down in the chair across the room, opening the newspaper to see just what was in the Peace Pointe Chronicle.

Peace Pointe, Florida, was a quiet town filled with restaurants, shops, and old people. As I flipped through the paper, I could see that reflected in its contents— coupons galore, a Health and Fitness section that focused this week on high cholesterol and took up nearly half of the paper, and a robust list of activities in town whose length was only rivaled by the obituary section.

Grandma put her phone next to her on the couch. "It's so sad to read about the budget cuts. I don't think people realize how much it's going to affect them. It has a trickle-down effect that people just don't think about. People lose their jobs, roads don't get fixed, school programs get cut, the police department has to cut back...it's just a bad situation all around."

I hadn't read anything about budget cuts so I flipped through the paper again and found a small article mentioning it on page two, right below an article about the benefits of square dancing.

"I can't believe you haven't mentioned anything

about your excitement this afternoon." Grandma smirked at me from across the room.

"How do you know about that?"

"I know about everything that happens in this town." She stood up and winked at me. "Don't go thinking this changes anything about you being in the meetings. If anything, it just proves this is a dangerous situation and I don't want you involved."

She walked in the kitchen to make some tea and I followed her. "Come on!" I protested. "I'm sure I can help in some way."

Grandma Dean put a kettle on the stove. "This is getting a little too high-profile for us. I'm not sure we'll even be able to help Artie Henson, especially if he can't control his anger."

"So, you're telling me you're just going to leave this to the police?"

"I'm saying there's a good chance we will. Now, what should we have for dinner?"

Grandma Dean opened the refrigerator and her phone rang in the living room. She casually disappeared to retrieve it and when she walked back into the kitchen, she was white as a sheet.

"What's wrong?" I asked, running to her.

She looked at me as tears filled her eyes. "Artie's dead."

IT DIDN'T TAKE LONG for the Grannies to arrive. I made enough tea for everyone and watched as one by one they trickled in, sniffling and hugging Grandma Dean.

"What happened to him?" Grandma Dean asked the group.

"Artie and Stan were at *Pastrami Pete's*. They had just left the police station after they gave their statements." Greta got choked up and put her hand to her mouth to hold back the sobs that wanted to escape. "Virginia and I were there."

Virginia reached around and looped Greta's arm in hers. "We didn't see it happen, thankfully. The guys passed us on their way to their table and said hello. Since it's such a beautiful day, they were going to sit outside."

"I just had my hair done," Greta cried. "Otherwise, we would've sat out there too."

"All the sudden, we heard this pop-pop noise. Then there was screaming. We rushed to the patio and Artie was on the ground, bleeding from his chest." Virginia could barely get the words out.

"He died with a pickle in his hand." Greta sobbed and Virginia pulled her close to comfort her.

Hattie gave a tsk-tsk sound. "No one should die with a pickle in their hand. That's picnic food, for goodness sakes!"

Virginia continued, "We followed the ambulance to the hospital and we weren't there long when we found out he didn't make it. We called you from the hospital."

It was silent for a minute while everyone took in the news. I suddenly felt guilty for wishing the car had hit him earlier. "I saw him at the coffee shop today. I was there when someone nearly ran over him."

"We know," Irene said, pulling out her phone. "He texted us and told us what happened while Detective Owen drove them to the police station. He said 'Poodles' was there too so, we all just assumed that was you."

She handed me her phone and sure enough, there was the text with a picture of a poodle emoji at the end of it. My guilt quickly faded away.

"We've got to get this SOB," Hattie said, pounding the table with her wrinkled fist. "He took out one of our own. Nobody messes with a retiree and gets away with it!"

Grandma Dean cleared her throat loudly and made a quick nod in my direction.

"Oh come on!" I yelled. "Let me stay! I can help!"

"I'm sorry," Grandma Dean said sympathetically. "We need to discuss this in private."

I sighed and started toward the living room door that led outside to the pool. That was usually where I was exiled during one of Grandma's meetings.

"Hold on, honey," Virginia called from the kitchen.

I came back in and stood by the table while she searched through her purse.

"I have something in here…" She rummaged around and pulled out a little container. "Here, hold out your hand." I did and she poured out a few green Tic Tacs. "There you go," she said, smiling. "You can freshen your breath a bit while you're out there!"

Gee, thanks.

"Oh, I have something too!" Greta reached for her white, leather bag and pulled out a package of Hostess Cupcakes. Now we were talking!

"Wait, wait!" yelled Hattie. "Here, in case you get thirsty!" She handed me a tiny can of prune juice. I secretly shuddered.

Irene searched her bag and gave me a stick of nicotine gum and a horoscope magazine.

"Thanks," I said halfheartedly, making my way to the back door and out to the pool.

I sat in a lounger and was relieved that Lloyd, the resident ladies' man, wasn't anywhere in sight. If he wasn't going on dates with the women, he was sitting by the pool in his speedo and silk robe. My heart sank when I saw him walk out of his door and head my way.

"Hello there, gorgeous!" He took a seat next to me and eyed my granny gifts. "You going to chew that?" he said, pointing to the gum.

I handed it to him. "I didn't know you were a smoker."

He popped the gum into his mouth. "I'm not. But I accidentally got hooked on the stuff a few years ago."

I laughed. "How did you get hooked on nicotine gum?"

He leaned back in his lounger and opened his silk

robe to the sun. I grimaced and turned away.

"Irene used to smoke and always wanted a cigarette after sex. But then when she quit and went to the gum, she'd pop a piece and offer me one."

"So, you took it?!"

"Of course. I wasn't going to look weak in front of my lady!"

I just shook my head. To each his own, I guessed.

"Good times," he said, smacking his gum loudly. "Goooood times."

Thankfully, Grandma Dean opened her door and motioned for me.

"Gotta go, Lloyd," I said, getting up quickly.

"But..." he stammered as he sat up. "We just started to talk."

"Sorry," I said, walking away. Then I turned to him. "Here, you can have this." I tossed him the prune juice.

"Oh!" he said happily. "It's the good brand!"

I quickly made my way to Grandma, who was still standing in the doorway. "Your meeting over all ready?"

"I just wanted you to know that we're stepping out for a little while. I don't know when I'll be back, so you'll have to have dinner on your own."

I peered around her. The Grannies were all waiting for her at the front door.

As I watched her walk away, a pinch of worry gripped my stomach. I didn't know exactly what she was up to, but I knew it probably wasn't good...or safe.

CHAPTER 4

Grandma Dean didn't get home until around midnight. I had been worried sick about her and when she came in, I was like a mother angry with her daughter for missing curfew. "Where were you? I've been worried sick, pacing these floors and wondering what could've happened to you! The least you could've done was answered one of my texts!"

"Sorry," she said, throwing her purse on the counter and walking to the sink to pour herself a glass of water. She opened a cabinet and pulled out a bottle of painkillers. I had been living there two months and I had never seen her take any kind of medication.

"Are you okay?" I asked.

She swallowed two pills. "I'm fine. Just a little out of practice for the kind of snooping around we did tonight."

"Did you find anything?"

"Nothing." She sighed and sunk down at the kitchen table. "Virginia and Greta are still out looking. They can't let this thing go. They're pretty shook up about it."

Grandma stood up and rubbed her face. She looked exhausted. "I'm heading to bed. The funeral is on Thursday if you want to go."

THE NEXT MORNING, we were up early and headed to our shop downtown. We were both feeling a little glum, but our spirits lifted as soon as we walked in the store. The bright white and pink interior filled us both with happiness and soon we were working, getting our store ready for the grand opening in a few days.

After a little while, Grandma disappeared and came back with something in her hand.

"This came for you yesterday," she said, handing me an envelope. "I'm sorry I didn't give it to you right away. I completely forgot about it after what happened to Artie."

"That's okay," I said, taking the envelope. I looked down to see who it was from and felt my breath leave my lungs. It was from Bo.

I looked up at Grandma Dean, who was standing there watching me. "If it's okay with you, I think I'll read this outside."

"Of course," she said with a soothing smile as she moved aside so I could get past her.

I walked out into the morning sunshine and noticed a bench two stores down. I made my way over and sat down, holding the envelope in front me, afraid to open it. This must be a reply to the letter I had sent him two weeks ago.

A few weeks ago, I had looked him up on one of his social media pages and saw a picture of him with Darcy McGee. She had her arm around him and they were smiling. I was furious when I saw it. He was my fiancée and he was supposed to wait for me while I figured things out in Florida. But it looked like he had quickly moved on. I wrote him a letter and told him how hurt I was. Of course, I left out my kiss with Joe and my date/not date with Detective Owen.

I slid my finger under the sealed flap and pulled out the folded piece of paper. When I saw his handwriting, something in my heart twisted. I didn't know what the letter would say, but I already had tears in my eyes. I missed him.

Nikki, I was so happy to get a letter from you. It's been difficult not reaching out to you but I wanted you to have your space to figure things out. I was a little surprised about your anger toward Darcy. You remember that she's my cousin, right? She's getting married and we all met at the Wooden Pickle to celebrate. You would've had a great time. After a few beers we had a darts competition and Trevor took a dart to the butt. We all had a good laugh. We talked about you a lot. Everyone misses you but I don't think anyone misses you as much as I do. I love you Nikki. I hope you're doing well in Florida. I know I shouldn't say this but I hope you come home soon.

Love, Bo

I felt like such a fool. I had completely forgotten that Darcy was his cousin. He handled it so well. I would've been furious if I had gotten the kind of letter I sent him. He was more mature than I was, that was for sure.

I reread the letter and couldn't help but laugh about Trevor's little accident. He was my brother-in-law, married to my sister Amber, and I couldn't stand him. The feeling was mutual. He was the one thing in Illinois I was happy to get away from.

I held the paper to my nose and breathed in, hoping to catch even a hint of Bo's scent. Suddenly, something caught my attention just over the top of the letter. The same guy that I caught staring at me the day before was staring at me now from across the street!

I slammed the letter down on my lap and the mystery guy took off down the street. This was getting weird. I tucked the letter back in the envelope and walked back to our store.

"Everything okay?" Grandma called after me when I walked in.

I shrugged. "I guess so, other than the fact that I'm a complete idiot."

"What did you do now?" Grandma Dean laughed.

"Remember that girl I saw Bo with in that picture? Well, it turns out it was his cousin."

Grandma cringed.

"I know. Thankfully, Bo was very nice about it." I handed her the letter and when she giggled, I knew she got to the part about Trevor. She knew we had a bad relationship, she just didn't know why. No one did and I intended to keep it that way.

"So, what now?" Grandma said, handing the letter back to me.

"I don't know," I whined. "I'm even more confused now than ever." I sat down on a white loveseat outside the little fitting room and put my head in my hands. Grandma Dean came over and sat next to me.

"I know that you love him," she started slowly, "but it also seems that maybe you've developed some feelings for Joe...and possibly Detective Owen."

My head shot up. "I do not have feelings for Detective Owen!"

"Okay, okay. Maybe not him. But do you have feelings for Joe?"

I sighed. "Maybe. I don't know." I put my head back in my hands. "Why do I keep doing this?" I mumbled through my hands. "Why can't I just be like everyone else and find a guy and settle down?"

"I don't know," she said, rubbing my back. "I think you need to take time and figure that out."

"Now you sound like my mother," I said, lifting my head to look at her.

"Well, mothers are pretty wise. As a matter of fact, the only thing wiser is a grandmother."

Grandma Dean smiled.

"Is there anything wiser than a grandmother?" I asked.

"God," she replied. "And that's about it."

———

THURSDAY CAME QUICKLY. Grandma Dean had continued to sneak out at night with the Grannies, but always came back emptyhanded.

With Kitty Purry's approval, we were out the door and headed to Holstein and Brachs Funeral Home. Grandma Dean had done my hair and makeup, and I looked more like I was going to prom than a funeral. Her look was understated and demure. Mine was more like nineties prom queen. It wasn't entirely her fault. Thanks to the high heat and humidity, my hair was resisting even her strongest concoctions.

"Good Lord, Baby Jesus, and Mother Mary," Hattie said when she saw me get out of Grandma's car at the funeral home. "You look like you just stepped out of the nineties. Where's your Zima?" I had no idea what Zima was, but Grandma Dean and Irene laughed.

"Oh, be nice to her," Grandma Dean said. "It's the best we could do with that hair. Once it was like that, I figured we might as well finish off the look."

"I just love funerals," Hattie said as we walked up to the building. "They make me feel so alive."

"I'm so thankful this one is going to be a closed casket. I think they learned their lesson with Simon Davidson. The poor guy was run over with a garbage truck. No amount of makeup was going to fix that up. I don't care if your last job was doing makeup for Tammy Faye Bakker." Irene opened the door for us and we walked in.

"Ugh," Hattie said immediately. "They changed the scent of their carpet deodorizer."

Grandma Dean and Irene sniffed. "They sure did," Grandma said, signing her name in the register. "I bet Mr. Holstein will get several complaints about that."

There was a surprisingly large turnout for Artie Henson's funeral. I scanned the room for anyone that I might know but was disappointed. I hadn't talked to Joe since our coffee date, but I was hoping that he might stop by.

I stood off to the side while Grandma mingled. The low hum of voices and soft music nearly put me to sleep and I found myself struggling to keep my eyes open. Then all the sudden, I got that strange feeling again like someone was watching me. I cautiously opened my eyes and looked around. There, in the opposite corner of the room, was the guy I had caught staring at me two different times downtown.

I made eye contact with him and he got clearly flustered and walked away. I decided to find out who this guy was. I walked up to Grandma Dean, who was having a discussion with a couple who I assumed to be husband and wife.

"Oh, here she is," Grandma Dean said when she saw me. "Greg, Betsy, this is my daughter's daughter, Nikki."

I inwardly rolled my eyes. She never called me her granddaughter in public because she said it made her sound old. Also, I was banned from calling her Grandma in public. She had a list of names I could use instead, but I refused to call her Coco, Peaches, or Mimmy. So usually, if I remembered, I would call her by her first name, Geraldine.

"Hello," I said, smiling at Greg and Betsy. "It's nice to meet you."

"Greg here is on the city council and was just telling me about some exciting things happening in our town."

"Oh, that's great. Hey, umm, can I talk to you for a minute in private?"

Grandma excused herself and walked with me out of the room. "Thank you so much for rescuing me," she said when we were out of earshot. "That man is absolutely dreadful. He has no idea what's actually good for this town."

We walked into the bathroom and I did a quick search under the stalls. We were alone. "Grandma, I caught some guy staring at me the other day when I was working in the shop and then I just saw him here and caught him watching me too."

"Oh, it's probably nothing," Grandma said, applying lipstick. "You're worrying over nothing."

"Grandma, we're at a funeral for a guy who was murdered. I think we should take everything a little more seriously."

"Do you know what I'm worried about?" Grandma Dean asked, looking at me in the mirror. "Greta and Virginia. They aren't here yet. Come on. Let's go see if we can find them."

With that, our conversation was over and she was pulling me out the door. Hattie and Irene met us right outside the bathroom with serious expressions.

"What's wrong?" Grandma asked.

"Virginia and Greta just got here. They said they wanted to show us something but we have to go now before it gets too dark." We started heading to the door and as we walked through the foyer, I saw my little stalker again.

I pulled on Grandma's arm. "Grandma, that's him. That's the guy that keeps staring at me!"

She looked in the direction I was nodding and smiled. "Oh, that's Les. He's harmless."

I had heard that one before but had quickly learned that "harmless" usually meant they had a secret we hadn't learned yet.

"Come on," Grandma said. "We can talk about Les later."

With that, we were heading out of the funeral home and piling into Virginia's SUV.

"My goodness. It has to be a hundred degrees in this car," Irene said as she climbed in. "I get so sick of this heat. One of these days, I'm going to move to Alaska."

The other Grannies agreed as we buckled ourselves in. We pulled out of the parking lot and turned onto the main road in front of the funeral home.

"What's that?" Greta asked, leaning forward and squinting, still fanning herself.

At first, I didn't see what she was talking about, but as we got closer, I gasped. There was a man lying face first on the sidewalk. We let out a scream in unison, then jumped out of the vehicle when Virginia pulled over.

"Stand back! I know what to do," Hattie yelled. "I've seen all fourteen seasons of *Grey's Anatomy*!"

"Oh, for Pete's sake," Grandma said, pushing her aside. "The man needs CPR, not a tracheotomy!"

Grandma did CPR while Irene called 911. Within minutes, a fire truck arrived followed by an ambulance. I was happy to see Joe get out. He and a paramedic rushed over to the man, and we all stood back while they got to work. Soon the poor guy was loaded onto a stretcher and disappeared into the back of the ambulance.

"Looks like it was just heatstroke," Joe said to the Grannies as he walked over to us. "That was quick thinking, Geraldine." She smiled with pride and the Grannies climbed into the SUV.

"I'm glad Hattie didn't do a trach on that guy like she did on the last one," Joe said to me, laughing.

"Oh my gosh! She actually did that?"

"Yep, but she's getting pretty good at it. Much better than she was a few years ago when she first tried it."

I cringed.

"Come on!" Irene yelled at me through the window. "We're losing daylight!"

"Sorry," I said to Joe. "We're on official business. I'll call you later."

He winked at me and I climbed in the vehicle before Virginia squealed her tires and drove away. My stomach turned a little, not knowing what we were headed into. Before, I couldn't wait to be included in one of the Grannie's adventures, but now, as we drove down Cranston Boulevard at breakneck speed, I was thinking maybe I wasn't cut out for this.

CHAPTER 5

ACROSS THE STREET FROM *PASTRAMI PETE'S* WAS A GAS station. Virginia turned off the main road and slowly drove past it. "We've been searching this area for where the shooter might have been," Virginia said, tapping on the window toward the side of the gas station. "The police say he was shot from somewhere across the street, though they haven't been able to pinpoint exactly where."

"We've canvassed this whole area," Grandma said, leaning toward Virginia's side of the car to peer out her window.

"Yes, quite thoroughly, but today, on the way to the funeral home, Greta and I decided to take one more look. We decided this time to walk a little further down the street."

Virginia pulled the vehicle over on the side of the road in front of a house that was for sale. The house appeared empty and it looked like the lawn hadn't been mowed in weeks. The bushes that snaked the front of the house were unruly, as were the cluster of bushes by the sidewalk.

The women got out of the car and stood in front of the house.

"You think someone stood this far away from *Pastrami Pete's* and managed to hit his target?" I squinted, trying to make out the people sitting on the patio of the restaurant nearly a block away.

"Oh please," Hattie said. "I could make that shot with my eyes closed."

Irene huffed, acting like she was offended by my statement. "I think we all could."

"Well, we know for a fact he was here." Virginia pointed to the bushes, leading us around them and into the yard. "Look, from this side you can see an area in the middle there where the branches are broken. That would be the perfect spot for someone to crouch down and hide. He...or she...could've shot through the bushes and hit Artie down the street."

"I'm not sure an impression in the bushes proves the shooter was sitting here," I commented, though the space was big enough for a person, as long as they weren't too big, to sit and be hidden.

"Look here," Greta said, grabbing a stick from the yard and pulling back the bushes.

The ladies gasped.

THE ROOT OF ALL EVIL

"Well, that definitely proves it." Grandma bent over to look at the shiny object—a bullet casing.

"That's not all. Look at this." Greta moved the stick and pulled back another area of the bushes. Everyone leaned in to get a closer look.

"What is that?" I asked, leaning over the bushes and squinting.

"It's a business card and what looks like a small piece of paper folded up." Virginia pulled out her phone. "We didn't want to touch it in case there were prints on it, most likely those things fell out of the shooter's pocket while he was crouched down in here, so I took a picture of it with my phone. If you look…" Virginia moved her fingers across the screen, zooming in on the card. "You can see clearly the company name on the card."

"That's interesting," Grandma said when the phone got around to her. "We need to let the police know what you found." Grandma handed the phone back to Virginia and pulled out her own phone. "I'll call Detective Owen. Virginia, why don't you text Stan and tell him to stop by my apartment after the funeral. We'll let him know what you found."

Within minutes, Detective Owen arrived at the scene. I stood back as the Grannies showed him their find. It wasn't long before more officers arrived, taping off the area and taking pictures of the bushes.

"I don't know how your grandmother does it." I

spun around to see Detective Owen standing behind me.

I laughed. "Yeah, she's pretty amazing. Her and her...card club."

This time, it was Owen who laughed. "That's one heck of a card club."

For some reason, I felt nervous standing in front him, guilty almost. Did he just have that effect on everyone or was I actually guilty of something? I tried not to notice how good he smelled, or admire his thick hair or his beautiful blue eyes. I was doing it again, spiraling into some kind of infatuation. Then I remembered how he tried to convict Grandma Dean when her shop burned down a few weeks before and I snapped out of it.

"Well, I better get back over there," Detective Owen said. "I just thought I'd come over here and say hi."

"Hi," I said lamely.

He laughed again and turned and walked away, back toward the bushes and all the secrets they held.

Grandma and the Grannies yelled from the sidewalk. "Come on, we're leaving!"

I stole one last glance at Detective Owen, who was now crouched beside the bushes, pointing at something. Even if I did have feelings for him, I had a feeling they wouldn't be returned. A serious guy like that wouldn't see anything interesting about an unserious girl like me.

BY THE TIME we picked up Grandma's car at the funeral home and made it back to her house, it was nearly nine o'clock. Grandma Dean looked through her cabinets trying to find some decaffeinated tea.

"I thought I had some in here somewhere." She stood on her tiptoes and checked another shelf. She pulled out a box of Earl Gray and put it on the counter next to the green tea. "It's too late in the evening to drink this stuff." I didn't think it was that big of a deal. It wasn't not like it was that late.

There was a knock on the door and the Grannies let themselves in. Irene and Hattie held cup carriers with tall cardboard cups sticking out of the top. "We picked up some hot tea on the way here. We decided on herbal peach since it's so late." Irene handed out the cups. "It's one of the few decaffeinated teas *Steamin' Beans* carries." Grandma threw the carriers in the recycling bin and we all sipped our tea. I wasn't a huge fan of hot tea, but it was pretty good.

"This one here is for Stan," Irene said, sitting down. "I wonder how he's doing with all of this. I haven't talked to him since Artie died. He hasn't taken a single one of my calls."

Greta sipped her tea. "Virginia and I paid him a visit the day after the accident and he was really upset and said he wanted to be alone."

Hattie looked around the room, then put her cup

down with force. "Well, if the rest of you aren't going to say it, I will. Artie was a rotten human being and I could never figure out why him and Stan were friends to begin with."

"Hattie, please," Grandma said in shock. "A man is dead. Let the poor guy be in the ground before you talk bad about him."

The other Grannies nodded in agreement. "Sorry," Hattie said, looking shamed. "I just couldn't stand the guy."

"Me either," Irene whispered to her.

"I couldn't either," Greta added under her breath.

"None of us could stand him, God rest his soul," Grandma said. "But him and Stan were friends, so obviously, Stan saw something in him we didn't."

"I don't understand it," I admitted. "For someone with no friends or family, there were a lot of people at his funeral."

"Nikki," Irene said seriously. "People don't go to funerals because they like someone. They go so people will go to *their* funeral."

"That's true." Hattie nodded. "Remember Iris? She never went to a single funeral and how many people were at hers?"

"Twenty, tops," Irene said indignantly. "Of course, we were there because we're good people."

"Yes, we are," Grandma Dean agreed. "Now, do any of you have any theories we should discuss before Stan gets here?"

Everyone was quiet so I spoke up. "What about that Les guy?"

"He didn't do it," Grandma said, cutting the conversation short.

"Les? Les who?" Hattie asked.

"Les…Sam and Aria's son."

"Oh, he didn't do it." Hattie said.

"How can you be so sure?" I asked. "I think he's been stalking me lately! He always seems to be around."

"It's always the quiet ones," Greta interjected. Her comment was met with dirty looks from the Grannies. "But he didn't do it," she said quickly.

"Honey, he probably likes you. He's a quiet fellow and he probably doesn't know how to express himself." Irene looked over her cup. "You have a thing with men, right? Maybe you've just pulled him into your web accidentally. Even spiders catch bugs they don't want."

Ouch.

"She's not a spider," Grandma scolded. "That's my daughter's daughter you're talking to. True, she's made some very ill choices when it comes to men, and yes, she continues to make mistakes here…" Grandma Dean looked at me with pity. "I really don't know where else to go from here."

"Thanks for trying," I mumbled, taking a sip of my tea. Grandma patted my arm.

There was a knock on the door and all the Grannies jumped in unison and walked to the door. "It must be Stan!" Hattie reached up and fluffed her hair.

Grandma Dean opened the door and a weary Stan walked inside. "We got you some tea," Hattie said, ushering him to sit next to her.

"Thanks," he said with his head down. "I'm not really hungry."

"Thirsty," Hattie corrected.

Stan looked up and finally paid attention to what Hattie was saying. "Oh, yeah, sorry. I'm not thirsty."

To Hattie's disappointment, he took a seat by Grandma. Everyone had to shuffle down a seat to make room for him.

Virginia patted him gently on the back. "How are you holding up?"

Stan sighed. "I just feel so bad. I know a lot of people didn't like Artie, but still, to kill him? In broad daylight? And no one even knows who did it." He looked up hopefully. "Do you ladies know who did it? Did you hear something?"

"Virginia and Greta found something tonight," Grandma informed him. "They've been tirelessly looking for clues and we think they found one."

"We found the bullet casing," Greta said proudly. "And a business card."

Stan didn't look impressed.

"It's a start," Grandma reassured him. "At least we know where the shooter took his shots and the police are looking for other evidence right now."

Stan hung his head again.

"Can you tell us anything that might be helpful? Did

he have any enemies..." Grandma stopped quickly and her face turned red.

Hattie laughed and said under her breath, "That's like asking if the Pope's classic."

"I think you mean Catholic," Irene corrected.

"I'm pretty sure it's classic...that's like asking if the Pope's classic...yeah, I'm pretty sure that's right."

"How could it be classic? That doesn't even make sense," Greta questioned.

"Yes, it does." Hattie pulled out her phone and typed something. "Here," she said, sitting up straight and pointing to her phone. "It says right here on the Merriam Webster website, 'judged over a period of time to be of the highest quality and outstanding of its kind.' That's the Pope!"

"I'm Catholic and I can tell you the saying is not 'classic'," Virginia said with irritation.

"Anyway..." Grandma gave them all a stern look. "Stan, was there anyone that you know of that was out to get him?

Stan seemed lost in his thoughts, which I was very thankful for. Hopefully, he missed the whole "classic" conversation. Finally, he shook his head. "Not really, I mean, you ladies know he wasn't well liked because of his..."

"Mouth," Hattie interjected.

We all glared at her for a minute. I thought Grandma was seconds from throwing her out the door.

"Well, yes," Stan agreed. "I was going to say disposition, but I suppose that works too."

Hattie just couldn't let this go. "Why were you even friends with him?"

Stan sat up straight. "I guess because he was a loner like me. Neither one of us had any kids. Our wives have been gone for years." He sighed. "When I moved here a few years ago, we just clicked. We were just two people without people."

"And I suppose he was nicer around you than he was in public," Virginia said, reaching out to pat his back again.

"Not really. He was awful pretty much all the time. But if you put him in front of a John Wayne movie and gave him a beer, he was tolerable."

There was silence around the table as everyone mulled over what to say next.

Grandma continued the gentle questioning. "What about money? Did he owe anyone anything? Loans? Gambling? Anything that might provoke someone to hurt him?"

"He was loaded," Stan admitted. "He didn't want anyone to know that, but he was. He owns the land on the east side. You know that whole farming area?" The Grannies nodded. "He owns it all. About a year ago, some builder came to him and wanted to buy it to put up a bunch of high-end condos."

Grandma and the Grannies suddenly became very alert.

"Did he sell?" Grandma asked.

"No, but the guy had the whole thing planned out and wasn't going to let it go. They even had their architect picked out—Larry Kramer, Lloyd's son. Well, if he hadn't decided not to sell it all ready, that would've sealed the deal. He can't stand Lloyd."

The Grannies looked at each other, each sitting at the edge of their seat by now.

"Stan," Grandma said, putting her hand on his. "When we said we found a business card at the scene of the crime… It was Larry's."

Stan leaned forward and put his head in his hands.

Now we were getting somewhere.

CHAPTER 6

WHEN STAN LEFT, EVERYONE WAS HEAVYHEARTED. Seeing Stan so upset took its toll on all of us. At least we finally had a motive. We said good-bye to the ladies then Grandma and I sat back down at the table.

"I think maybe we should postpone the grand opening of our shop," Grandma said. "I just don't feel like I can focus on it right now."

I felt bad. I knew how much our shop meant to her.

"You focus on the investigation and I'll focus on the shop," I reassured her. "If we have to push back our grand opening a day or two, that's okay, but I really think we can still open on time."

"But I wanted to work on it with you," she objected. "And other than the one day when you and I went in, you've done it all yourself."

"We'll have plenty of time to work together once it's open. It will be fine, I promise."

Grandma smiled at me and patted my hand. "You're a good granddaughter."

"You mean I'm a good daughter of your daughter?" I said with a wink.

"Yes, that too," she laughed. "Well, I suppose we should get some rest. It's been a long day. You head to the shop in the morning and I'll get together with the ladies and see if we can come up with a plan."

"You know I'm here if you need me," I reminded her.

"I know." She smiled and patted my hand again. "If you get up early enough, I'll do your hair. I'm sorry I couldn't do much with it earlier today. That thing has a mind of its own."

After I told Grandma good night, I went to my room and sat on my bed. Catalie Portman squeezed through the nearly closed door and joined me. "What a day," I confided in her. "You're lucky you're a cat." She purred and I stroked her fuzzy little brown head. I sighed. I was exhausted and irritable, so I decided now would be a good time to call my mother. Usually, I felt like that after I talked to her—might as well start out that way.

She answered on the third ring, worry evident in her voice.

"Are you okay? Why are you calling so late? Is it your grandmother?"

"Mom, everything's fine." I glanced at the clock

beside my bed. 10:30. Was that too late to call? "I just had a minute and I thought I'd check in."

She breathed a sigh of relief. "Oh, well everything is fine here—except for Trevor. He's off work for a week because of his accident."

"Oh, yeah. I heard about that. Bo told me about it in his letter."

Mom sighed again. "That man! He went to that bar even though your sister told him not to and look what happens! Some drunk guy hits him in the butt with a dart! Somebody got it all on camera and now the whole worlds gets to see him scream like a girl and watch Reverend Barns pull a dart out of his butt cheek."

"Reverend Barns was there?" I asked, surprised.

"He was there to hang some flyers about the bake sale on the bulletin board when Trevor was hit. I'm so embarrassed I could practically die. Then, to make matters worse, him and your sister came to dinner one night and said it went viral! I said, 'you better get an antibiotic for that or you're going to be in big trouble!'"

"Mom," I said gently. "I don't think that's what they meant when they said it went viral."

"Well, whatever they meant, two days later, he's at the urgent care with an infection that went clear to his hip bone!"

"Yikes," I cringed. "That doesn't sound good."

"It's not." I thought I heard her sniff. "He's off work for a week and your dad and I are helping out with money right now. It's not like we can't afford to help them, it's just... Wait, did you say you got a letter from Bo?"

I was surprised by how quickly the conversation turned and I wasn't ready for the topic to be about Bo. "Yeah," I replied casually, "but finish what you were saying about Trevor."

To my disappointment, her rant about Trevor was over.

"Bo was at dinner last week and said he was going to write you back…"

"He was at dinner? At your house?"

"Well, of course, he eats with us every Sunday. And how could you forget Darcy was his cousin? Everyone in town knows that."

I didn't know what to say first. 'Why is my fiancé, the one I'm still trying to decide if I want to marry, at your house every week for dinner, or how in the world can I keep up with everyone's cousin in a small town where everyone is related?'

My mom decided to chime in instead.

"I'm sorry I'm not myself tonight. I don't know what's wrong with me. I'm just tired, I guess. I don't mean to complain so much. And if you don't want us to have Bo here for dinner anymore…"

"No," I interjected. "I don't want you to stop inviting him over. If you want to have him over for dinner then you should. I just didn't realize that was happening."

"Well, your dad and I figured it was a way to make things easier for him after you left. We assume you'll come back and marry him…but if you decide not to, at least we know we did what we could to make things okay here at home for the time being."

"That's very nice of you." Suddenly, I felt terrible. I never thought about how my decisions effected my parents. I always thought it was my life and my decisions and it shouldn't matter to them what I did. But it did matter. Just like it mattered that Trevor had a butt infection. And most likely him and my sister were having some marital problems if he went to a bar and she didn't want him to. My mom had a big heart and all of this was weighing on her.

"You're a good mom," I told her. "I don't tell you that enough."

I heard her sniff again. "Thank you," she said quietly.

I hung up the phone wondering why we don't say things like that very often. Why don't we praise the people who raised us, or the spouses or significant others who put up with us, or even the people who bag our groceries, or deliver our mail? I guess it's because we feel like that's their job. They're just doing what they're supposed to be doing. But really, we have no idea the inner turmoil they go through because of us. I made up my mind to try to be more thankful—not just inwardly, but outwardly. Life wasn't all about me and I needed to start living like it.

GRANDMA DEAN WENT ALL OUT on my hair the next morning. My naturally curly hair didn't have a frizz in sight. I reached up and touched it, expecting my hair to be crunchy, but instead it was soft and my hair was bouncy. It was the kind of hair you only dreamed was possible, and yet here it was, a reality.

She dropped me off in front of our store and promised to be back for me later. She was heading to a meeting with the other Grannies and told me she'd tell me all about it at lunch. As much as I wanted to go with her, I knew my working at the shop would ease her mind a little. I reminded myself of my promise the night before to think more about others and that helped lessen my disappointment a little.

It was eight in the morning and, armed with a coffee with enough cream to make butter, I was ready to get to work.

The more I worked, the more I realized just how much I enjoyed it. The shop was cheerful and bright, and sunlight poured in the large front windows. I hung bracelets and cat collars on a jewelry stand that looked like a tree, and clipped bows and barrettes with little cats on them to long strings of braided ribbon.

But my favorite part of the morning was getting the French corner set up. In the far-left corner, I put up a tall cardboard Eiffel Tower; two long mirrors flanked the side and a plush, pink rug sat in front of it. Two twirly stands stood on either side of the mirrors—one for berets and one for scarves, large ones for the people and small ones for the cats. I held a gray cat beret in my hand and chuckled. I wasn't sure who would want to have a matching beret and scarf with their cat, but if anyone did, we had them.

I had just finished with the scarf display and turned to see what was next on my to-do list when I caught that guy, Les, staring at me again through the windows. I narrowed my eyes at him and he quickly turned and took off. I ran to the front of the store and threw the doors open.

"Les," I called after him.

He turned and looked at me, surprised.

"Come here," I said, motioning him toward me.

He looked terrified, frozen in place, not sure what to do next.

"It's all right," I said sweetly. "Come on."

He took a few steps toward me, then stopped and looked around. I assumed he was checking his surroundings, looking for a quick escape route.

To my surprise, he didn't bolt. Instead, he cautiously made his way over to me. "How do you know my name?" he asked when he got about ten feet from me.

"The real question," I said with arms crossed, "is why are you stalking me?"

"I'm not stalking you," he said with a nervous laugh. "I was just trying to figure out…uh…what kind of shop this is going to be when it opens."

"Okay…" I played along. "So why were you staring at me at the funeral home?"

His face flushed, then he laughed. He ran his hand through his sandy hair. "You got me there."

I took a second and really looked at him for the first time. He was tall and lanky and needed a haircut. None of his features really stood out. I could tell he was socially awkward and talking to me was probably a big deal.

"Next time," I said to him, "just stop in and say hi. When you stare at me like that, it's creepy." I smiled to let him know I was saying this in a friendly way.

He smiled back. "Okay. I'll do that."

All of the sudden, a car swung into the parking space closest to me and came to a screeching halt. Les and I both jumped back, even though we were at a safe distance on the sidewalk. Grandma poked her head out the window. "Lock up," she hollered. "We have to go!"

I looked up at Les and shrugged. He smiled, then turned and took off running down the street.

What a strange guy, I thought.

"Hurry!" Grandma yelled.

I ran inside and did as I was told. I didn't know which unsettled me more—Les's odd behavior or Grandma's.

CHAPTER 7

"No, I'm not going to do it." I folded my arms and leaned back in the kitchen chair, looking at all the Grannies. "It's not going to happen."

"Come on," Greta coaxed. "It's for a good cause."

"No!"

Grandma leaned over in front of me. "What if we sweeten the pot? We'll give you a hundred dollars!"

"I'm not going to go on a date with Lloyd's son so you can sneak in his house and try to find evidence and that's final!" How could they even ask me to do such a thing!

"I see how it is," Irene said with her eyes narrowed. "You'll marry six men but you won't let your grandmother whore you out for one evening!"

"I'm not whoring her out," Grandma corrected. "I'm simply offering her money to go on a date with a man…" She scrunched up her face as she thought about

54

that for a moment. "Okay, change of plans, the money's off the table!"

I rolled my eyes.

"Look," Grandma said, softening her tone, "we need you. We've thought about this a hundred times and we just can't do this safely without you."

She had to say the ONE word that would get me to say yes—safely.

"Fine," I said, caving. "I'll do it."

The Grannies let out a whoop.

"But how are you going to get him to go out with me?"

"Already taken care of," Grandma said, walking over to the kitchen counter and rummaging through her purse. "I called him and told him you're new in town and would like to meet some new people. He was happy to take you out for the evening."

"You set this up before I even said yes?" I asked, not nearly as shocked as I tried to sound.

"Well, we try to be prepared for everything." Grandma smiled.

"What was your plan if I said no?"

The Grannies looked at each other. There was no plan.

"Here." Grandma handed me a tube of lipstick she just pulled out of her purse. "I bought you this for the occasion! It will go perfectly with the outfit we picked out for you."

I flipped the tube over and read the name of the

color. Crimson Tramp. I could only imagine what my outfit looked like.

THAT EVENING, I stood in front of the mirror and barely recognized the person looking back. My curly hair had been straightened and laid in long layers nearly down to my elbow. The short black dress that Grandma had given me hugged my body and the long, tight sleeves made my arms look thin and toned. But it was the shoes that were my favorite part of the outfit—black wedges that crisscrossed up my ankle. My makeup—subtle smoky eyes, a hint of bronzer, and some carefully placed highlighter—were topped off with my Crimson Tramp lips.

When Grandma Dean and I walked into the kitchen, the other Grannies' jaws dropped.

"Oh my stars!" Greta exclaimed. "You look like a model!"

"Or a movie star," Virginia added in shock.

I had to admit, I looked pretty darn good.

"Okay," Grandma said, giving me her keys. "Remember the plan—you're going to meet him at the *Cobbler's Tea Room* in thirty minutes. The girls and I are going to head to his house and wait for him to leave. As soon as he's gone, we'll sneak in and head to his office downstairs."

"Why can't he have an office in some building

downtown like everyone else around here?" Hattie complained.

"I have no idea," Grandma said sharply. "You can ask him that next time you see him."

"Okay, ladies, are we ready?"

The Grannies filed out and I took a deep breath. It was showtime.

I pulled up in front of the *Cobbler's Tea Room* and my stomach was doing flip-flops. I kept giving myself the same pep talk over and over. "You can do this, Nikki. You are brave, you are strong, you are beautiful." Unfortunately, I didn't believe any of it at that moment.

What would Grandma Dean do in this situation? I asked myself. She would get out of the car, march herself up to the restaurant, and charm the pants off Larry Kramer. Wait, poor choice of words. I needed to make sure Larry Kramer's pants stayed on.

Just as I was about to get out of the car, I got a text from a number I didn't recognize.

Hey it's Larry. Change of plans. Meet me at my house. 1862 Thornberry Heights. Come in the back gate.

Crap. This was not good. I quickly called Grandma Dean and told her the news. There was some chatter on the other end while they discussed what to do.

"Okay, just do it. He has a huge house, just try to keep him toward the back of it. Text me if something goes wrong."

I hung up and drove to his house with a terrible

feeling in the pit of my stomach. I hadn't even met the guy yet and already things were going wrong.

I found his street and pulled around to the back. Grandma Dean wasn't joking when she said he had a huge house. But I guessed that was to be expected on a street lined with houses that were the same size as elementary schools.

The gate was unlocked so I opened it and walked in. It was evening, but the yard was fairly well lit. I walked through the grass and up to the pool area. I stood on the sidewalk that wrapped around the pool and looked up at his house. Every light was on and you could see right in. I looked around to see if his neighbors could see into his house as well, but it seemed that his house was fairly well hidden by trees.

"Hey there. You must be Nikki." A man's voice made me jump back and I almost lost my balance thanks to my high wedges.

I looked around to see where the voice came from.

"Down here," he said.

I looked down and could see his head and shoulders sticking out of the pool. I took another step back, unsure what was happening.

"Feel like going for a swim?"

"Um, no thank you," I said, clearly uncomfortable with the situation.

Larry laughed. "I'll come out then."

He grabbed onto the ladder a few feet away and climbed out. I gasped. He looked like a barely younger, and less fit, version of his father—clear down to the speedo.

Larry ran his hand through his wet, black hair and arched his back like he thought he was being sexy. Water trickled down his shoulders, through his thick, dark chest hair and over his extended belly. Suddenly, I saw something move and as much as I tried to avert my eyes, I couldn't help but see a clump of lint wash out of his belly button.

"Do you like what you see?" he asked.

"Um, yes, your pool is amazing. It's like...Olympic size and everything."

He laughed and reached over to take my hand. "I'm Larry Kramer and you must be Nikki." He kissed my hand and when his lips lingered far too long, I pulled it away. He smiled. "Playing hard to get, I see. I like that." He winked at me then looked me up and down. "I have to say, I'm pleasantly surprised. You're not at all what I thought you'd look like."

"Oh?" I asked, a little offended. "And what did you expect?"

"Well," he laughed, "for someone whose nickname is Poodles, well, I just thought you'd be a little fluffier."

I wasn't sure if he meant my hair or my body, but either way, I didn't like it. Wait a minute! The only person who had called me Poodles was Artie!

"Would you like to go inside?" he asked. "I think we'll be more comfortable in there."

"No," I objected a little too forcefully. His eyes got

big and he was clearly surprised. I tried to dial it back a little. "It's just...so beautiful out here...so romantic." I nearly threw up.

He smiled. "It is, isn't it? Under the stars, with a gentle breeze. It's a night for lovers."

Keep it together, keep it together, I kept telling myself. I was doing this to keep Grandma safe, but who was going to keep me safe?

"Let's sit here for a while and you can tell me all about yourself." I motioned to the patio furniture that sat to our left.

Those were like magic words to him. He sat down and immediately started to gloat about his money and his business and all the material possessions he owned. I quickly texted Grandma Dean.

Hurry it up! I can't take much more of this! We're in the back by the pool. Don't know how long I can keep him out here.

She didn't respond and I started to feel antsy. Then something caught my eye. Thankfully, I was the one facing the house and not Larry, because the Grannies could be seen cavorting in the kitchen! I tried not to stare and bring attention to them, but I couldn't help but squint a little to make out what they were doing. Were they drinking? Yes! Hattie had a wine glass in her hand! How could they do this to me? I was out here with this creep and they were in his house drinking his wine and having a good ole time!

"What are you lookin' at, darlin'?" Larry asked and he started to turn around.

I panicked. If he turned around, he would see what I could see!

I grabbed him and kissed him on the lips. I fought back my repulsion and counted to five then tried to pull away. But he had other plans. He pulled me closer and I felt his tongue fight his way into my mouth. Once inside, it sat there like a dead slug. He made some weird humming noise and moved his head from side to side. This man did *not* know how to kiss. I looked past him and saw that the Grannies were no longer visible. I pulled away, using my hands against his chest as leverage. My hands disappeared into his chest hair and I quickly pulled them away.

Larry still had a strong hold on my upper arms and was smiling from ear to ear.

"Wow," he said. "Did you feel that spark? Because I definitely felt a spark. How about you and me go inside and turn that into a fire?"

"Actually," I said, wiggling free of his arms and standing up. "I suddenly don't feel very well. I think it was something I ate."

He stood up next to me, not convinced.

"Or maybe it's lady problems," I threw in. If that didn't work, I was not beneath telling him I had diarrhea...or herpes. Whatever it took to get out of there. Thankfully, that did the trick.

He grimaced. "Oh, well, call me in a few days and

we'll try this again." He tried to come in for another kiss, but I managed to back away just in time.

"You have a lovely home," I shouted over my shoulder as I practically ran through his backyard. "Have a good night!"

Once I was safely on the other side of the gate, I sent Grandma a text and told her I was out and she better be too. She texted back that they had just gotten in the car and were driving away and to meet her at home.

I shuddered and looked in the mirror. My lipstick was smeared across my face. I opened Grandma's glove compartment and pulled out a package of wet wipes and ran one along my lips. Then I opened my purse and grabbed the tube of lipstick Grandma bought me and tossed it out the window. No more Crimson Tramp for me.

CHAPTER 8

WHEN I PULLED ONTO THE STREET FOR THE GOLDEN Acres Retirement Community, my heart dropped. Red lights flashed up ahead. That was never a good sign, especially at a place like this. But as I got closer, I noticed there wasn't just an ambulance but several police cars. Virginia pulled in behind me and Grandma and her friends jumped out of the SUV.

"Oh, no," Greta whispered with her hand over her mouth. "What do you think happened?"

We scanned the crowd for someone we could ask. Suddenly, Grandma spotted Wanda Turnbough. "Wanda!" she yelled, motioning for her.

Wanda walked over and even in the dark, we could tell she was white as a sheet.

"What happened?" we all asked at once.

"Someone shot at Stan through his window." She was shaking and holding back tears.

"Oh my gosh!" Hattie cried. "Is he okay?"

"The bullet missed him, thankfully. But shards of glass flew everywhere and his arm is cut up pretty bad. And I think the poor guy about had a heart attack."

The ambulance turned on its sirens and sped out of the parking lot, leaving us all silent as we watched it leave.

"Are there any witnesses?" Grandma asked

Wanda shrugged. "I don't know. I know the police are questioning people, but honestly, I don't think anyone would've seen it. It's eight-thirty. No one is out that late."

Then Wanda eyed the Grannies and she let out a noise that stated her irritation. "Humph, I see you all were out, doing God knows what, while our poor Stan was nearly shot dead!"

Wanda and Grandma used to be friends, from what Lloyd had told me a few weeks ago. But when Wanda was denied admittance into the Glock Grannies, she was not happy about it. Lloyd said it was because Grandma didn't want anyone in the group younger than she was and, even though I never questioned her about it, I assumed it was true. That sounded exactly like something Grandma Dean would do. Apparently, Wanda was still holding a grudge.

"Maybe I'll just start looking into this myself," Wanda said with a huff. "I could probably do a better job than all of you!"

With that, she turned and stormed away.

"Well, someone has a bee up her…"

"Hattie!" Irene scolded. "Do you kiss your grandkids with that mouth?"

"What? I was going to say bonnet!" Hattie looked at me and whispered, "I wasn't actually going to say bonnet." She winked a sly little wink.

Grandma sighed. "Let's go see if we can get some more information from someone a little less irritable."

I stood there in the dark with the police lights flittering in the air and watched the Grannies wave down Lloyd. I decided to stay behind. I didn't want to be anywhere near another member of the Kramer family.

"Wow! Look at you!" a man's voice said, making me jump about five feet. "A little jumpy tonight?" he laughed.

It was Detective Owen. He walked up to me and casually put his hands in the pockets of his khakis. He seemed a bit too cocky for my liking.

"Well," I said defensively, "someone was shot here tonight. That can put a person on edge."

He gave a little nod like he agreed, then looked me up and down. "So, where have *you* been tonight?"

I sighed. "I'd rather not say."

Detective Owen became serious for a minute. "Nikki, I don't exactly know what your Grandma and her gang are up to, but I need you to convince them to stay out of this."

"Yeah, right," I laughed. "Like I could convince her

to not do something. That woman's mind is not easily changed."

"I know it's not…" He paused and looked me in the eyes. "Whoever we're dealing with here is extremely dangerous and I don't want you getting hurt."

The way he looked at me made my stomach do a little flip.

"I'll talk with her. But I can't guarantee anything."

"Good girl," he said, slapping me on the shoulder and walking away.

I narrowed my eyes at the back of his head. Good girl? Like I was some child…or a dog? That guy really annoyed me.

Before I had a chance to act on the heinous thoughts in my head, Grandma Dean came up and pulled my arm. "Come on, we're heading inside to talk about what we found tonight."

I let my own murderous thoughts go and followed Grandma and the other Grannies into the house. I knew there was no way I could discourage them from looking for Artie's murderer. And, knowing Owen was against it, just made me want to help them even more.

"So," Grandma said, sitting at the head of the table. "What did you find out tonight, Nikki? Anything useful?"

My mouth flew open in surprise. "What? I wasn't

supposed to find anything out! You were! My job was to distract Larry and your job was to do the snooping!"

"Well," Irene said with a huff, "a good undercover agent would've done both."

The Grannies all gave me a look like I had just stolen the last cookie from the cookie jar.

"That's okay," Grandma Dean said, patting the back of my hand. "It was your first time. You'll know better next time."

I sunk down in my chair feeling defeated.

They sat there quietly and didn't say anything. "Well, what did *you* find?" I finally asked, hoping to get the conversation started.

They looked at each other for a moment. "Not much," Grandma said, looking defeated herself.

Now we all sunk down in our chairs. This night was a total waste.

"Wait a minute," I said, sitting up straight. "So, what were you guys doing in Larry's kitchen tonight? Drinking and having a good time while I was out having the most miserable night of my life!"

Irene laughed. "No, we were covering our tracks."

"Any time we break in somewhere to do a little snooping, we always seem to accidentally leave something behind or some evidence that we were there —no matter how careful we try to be!" Greta explained. "So, we decided this time to just play that up. We made it look like we were one of Larry's ladies who snuck in for a little rendezvous and since she didn't see him, she left him a few gifts."

The Grannies laughed and I felt my blood go cold. "What kind of gifts?"

"Well, since I have the plumpest lips of the group, I got to be the one who left the lipstick mark on the wine glass." Hattie sat up proudly and stuck her lips out. The other Grannies rolled their eyes.

"What else did you do?" I asked, knowing that couldn't have just been the end of it.

"We put a bra from *Victoria's Secret* on his kitchen table!" Irene said with a laugh. "Right next to the wine glass! It's going to be eating him up for days trying to figure out who left it!"

"We bought a double-D just for fun! Really make him think!"

"You bought an expensive bra just to leave it there?" I asked.

"Well," Hattie spoke up. "We looked through your underwear drawer, but there was no way we were going to leave those rags in his house. We wanted to make him think someone was there to seduce him, not dust his end tables."

"You went through my drawer?" I turned to Grandma. "How you could you let them do that?"

"I told them they wouldn't find anything usable in there," she said defensively.

"That's not the point!" I practically shouted.

"Oh, calm down," Irene said. "It was a good thing we

did. We all decided to take you out bra shopping. Won't that be fun?"

Oh yes. Lots.

"They had so many cute ones, Nikki." Greta was all smiles. "I'm sure you'll find some you like! And you can get matching underwear! It will be a little thank you from us for having to go out with Larry tonight."

I sighed. It sounded like it was already decided then. And once the Grannies decided something, there was no going back.

"Well, thank you. I probably could use a few new ones."

"I really liked that store," Hattie said after taking a sip of her tea. "But I have no idea why it's called *Victoria's Secret*. Let me tell you, after seeing those large posters in there, I can tell you that nothing is a secret anymore!"

Irene shook her head. "And that lady that worked in there! How much do you think her boobs cost? Those were clearly not God-given! She must have spent a small fortune on them!"

"I bet you my boobs cost more than hers," Greta said with a gentle laugh.

Our mouths dropped in shock. "You've had your boobs done?" Virginia asked.

"No," Greta smiled. "But six babies made these boobs the way they are and I can tell you that ain't cheap. These boobs were made with love and sacrifice. That seems pretty priceless to me."

Sometimes, these women made me cringe and want to pull out my hair, and other times, times like this, I just wanted to hug them and glean all the granny wisdom I could from them. I hoped that one day I could learn to love myself like the Grannies did.

"I think we should tell Nikki what we found on Larry's table," Virginia said slowly.

"Virginia," Grandma Dean said with a scowl. "That has nothing to do with this case and you know it."

"I think we should tell her too," Greta agreed.

I looked from granny to granny waiting for someone to tell me something. No one wanted to be the one to defy Grandma. "Well, what was it?" I asked.

Grandma sighed. "We found a contract with Les's name on it. But he hasn't even signed it yet."

As interesting as I thought that was, it didn't really implicate Les in Artie's murder. Before I could say anything, Greta spoke up. "Tell her where the property is."

Grandma was clearly irritated, but she told me anyway. "It's right next to the property that Artie owns."

"It's for a condo!" Greta blurted out.

"This is Florida!" Grandma shouted. "There are about as many condos in this state as there are skin cancer doctors!" She looked at me sternly. "I can assure you, Les didn't do this. He's a nice, quiet guy. He wouldn't kill a spider, let alone a man."

Greta gave me a look that said she wasn't convinced.

"Besides," Grandma said, standing up and pacing the floor. "This doesn't add up. Now it's not just Artie they wanted dead...but Stan too. Why would someone want to kill both of them?"

The room was quiet while we all thought about it.

"Unless," Grandma said, her eyes popping open with an idea, "they weren't after Artie at all!"

"What do you mean?" Virginia asked. "Artie was the one that was always targeted. And then he was the one that was shot and killed!"

Grandma sat down and leaned across the table. "What if Stan was the murderer's intended victim all along, but he just has really bad aim! You heard what happened to Stan tonight! He was sitting in his chair in front of a window and the guy still managed to miss him!"

We took in Grandma's revelation for a moment and then the Grannies started to get excited. "I think you might be right, Geraldine!" Virginia said as she thought it over. "It makes sense! Everyone just assumed Artie was the target because he was so awful! No one ever would've thought it was really Stan the killer wanted!"

"All right, girls," Grandma said, standing again. "Tomorrow, we'll pay Stan a little visit and see why someone might be coming after him. Let's all get our rest. We're going to need it!"

CHAPTER 9

"Are you sure you're okay with this?" Grandma Dean asked as she dropped me off in front of our store.

"Of course," I assured her. "You can just swing by and pick me up later."

"We're going to have to push back our grand opening." Grandma was clearly disappointed by her decision. "I just can't focus on it when I have this investigation going on. I haven't even had a chance to do any advertising."

"It's okay. I'll finish getting the store ready and when things quiet down, we'll open."

She smiled at me and breathed a little sigh of relief. I had never seen her like this. I knew she was worried about Stan and, even though she hadn't really liked him, Artie's death was still difficult for her to deal with.

"The girls and I are going to check on Stan at the

hospital. They kept him overnight because they were afraid the scare affected his heart. We're going to figure out a safe place for him to stay. I'm going to meet with Detective Owen this afternoon and talk to him about Stan and the case. Do you think they'll put him in protective custody?"

I had no idea how that worked.

She shrugged. "Hopefully, I'll get some answers today."

I got out of the car and leaned down to talk to her through the open door. "I'll just eat at one of the restaurants down here so take your time."

"Thank you, Nikki," she said, looking weary.

I closed the door and watched her drive away. I was worried about her—and all of the Grannies, really. What if the killer wasn't just after Stan? What if he was knocking off the residents at the retirement village one by one? Who would be next? I shuddered and a chill ran up my spine. Suddenly, I felt a little paranoid. I looked around, but no one seemed to be watching me. I went into the store and locked the door behind me.

Around noon, I decided to take a break. I had just about finished everything on my list anyway. Another hour and our store would be ready for the grand opening...whenever that would be. Unfortunately, I didn't have another hour's worth of energy left in me.

As I walked outside and started to lock up, I glanced down the sidewalk and saw Les up ahead. I locked the door and hollered after him. He turned and looked, saw it was me and got flustered. I could tell he didn't know whether to stay frozen or bolt. Honestly, at that moment, I wouldn't have been surprised if he fell to the ground and played dead until I gave up and walked away.

I knew I needed to act fast if I didn't want to lose him. "Wanna grab some lunch?" I yelled.

He started to walk toward me, then stopped. I was sure he was questioning whether he heard me right.

"Are you free for lunch?" I asked as I walked toward him.

"You want to have lunch…with me?"

"Yes! What's good to eat downtown? The only place I've been is the coffee shop down the street."

He thought for a minute. "*Sally's* is good…if you like sandwiches."

"I love sandwiches," I said happily. "Lead the way!"

Our walk to Sally's was a quiet one. I tried to make small talk, but Les either didn't have anything to say or didn't know how to communicate. At this rate, it was going to be near impossible to get him to tell me why and how he planned to build a condo next to Artie's land.

Once we got to the restaurant and ordered, he seemed to relax a bit. We got our drinks and sat down at a table in the corner. The place was starting to fill up fast with the lunch rush. We had made it just in time.

Les set a notebook he had been carrying on the table next to him.

"What's that for?" I asked him.

He started to get nervous again and it only piqued my curiosity.

"You don't have to tell me," I finally said.

He let out a breath and sat back in his chair, obviously relieved.

"How long have you lived here?" I asked, trying again to make small talk.

"Pretty much my whole life," he answered. "We traveled a lot when I was a kid, but this was always home."

"Oh! Traveling! That sounds exciting! Where did you go?"

"Mostly Miami. But we made several trips to Chicago and St. Louis. A few times, we went to Milwaukee."

"To visit family?" I asked.

"No, it was for my dad's job."

"What did he do?"

Les fumbled with his napkin for a minute. He was really reluctant to share anything.

"Well, *my* dad's a farmer," I finally said. Maybe if I shared a little bit about my life, he'd open up about his. "And my mom was a stay-home-mom."

"Farms are fun," he said with interest. "Did you have animals?"

"Oh yes, lots of different ones. After I graduated

from high school, I went to work for a wealthy guy in our little town that had show horses. I took care of them, trained them, that sort of thing. I got to live in a cute little house on his property." Suddenly, I missed my little house and the horses…and Bo.

"You seem sad," Les said, looking me in the eyes for the first time since we sat down.

"I am a little, I guess. I'm just trying to figure out my future."

He sighed. "I understand that. I'm twenty-eight and I still don't know what I'm going to do with my life."

"What do you do right now?" I asked cautiously, trying to not pressure him.

"I own the record store across the street from your store."

Oh, that made sense, since every time he ran away from me he ran in there.

"That's exciting," I said sincerely.

"Yeah, it's okay. It's just not what I really want to do, you know what I mean?"

"What do you want to do?"

"I don't even know." He hung his head.

"Well, that's okay," I said brightly. "There's nothing that says you have to figure it out today."

He laughed. "I guess you're right."

"Do you have any family around here?" I asked, changing the subject to something hopefully less stressful.

"My parents moved away a few years ago," he answered. "I don't have any siblings."

The waitress came over and brought our food. My roast beef sandwich with cranberry mustard looked amazing, as did his barbeque chicken sandwich.

Once we started to eat, Les finally opened up. We started talking and sharing our ideas about businesses. Then we got back to the subject of his family.

"My grandma told me your parents' names are Sam and Aria. Aria is such a beautiful name. Is it a family name?"

He laughed. "Actually, when my parents met, my mom's name was Samantha but she went by Sam, and my dad's name was Aria. They decided to switch names when they got married."

"You have to be kidding me!"

"Nope, they are both creative types and they thought Aria fit my mom better as an artist and Sam fit my dad better as a comedian."

"Your dad is a comedian?" I asked, surprised.

"He was." Les wiped some barbeque sauce off his face. "Now my parents own an art gallery in downtown Austin."

"That's cool! Is your mom's artwork in it?"

"Yeah, and other local artists. They have art shows there and crazy dinners with food no one has ever heard of before. They love it." He stopped for a minute and was lost in thought. "I want to do something I love too. I just don't know what that is. Life is so much

77

more meaningful if you're doing what you love, don't you think?"

I had never really thought about it before.

"So how did you get the name Les?" I asked. "Is that like your grandpa's name or something?"

Les turned nervous again. What was with this guy?

"No," he said slowly. Then he sighed. "I might as well tell you. My name is actually Lesus."

"What's wrong with that?" I asked, sticking a house-made potato chip in my mouth. Those things were addictive.

He took a deep breath like he was going to tell me something that might possibly blow me away or make me go running for the hills. What it actually did was make me laugh and choke on my chip.

"Are you okay?" he asked, jumping up and running over to my side of the table. I took a drink of my soda.

"I'm fine," I coughed.

He sat back down, his face red in embarrassment.

"I'm so sorry," I apologized. "I didn't expect you to say Moore. Why would your parents do that to you?"

He shrugged. "They are the artsy type. Always thinking outside the box. They believed in a minimalist lifestyle—probably because in the beginning, they couldn't afford much—and that was their saying. Less is more. When they decided to have kids, they only wanted one. They decided to go for quality over quantity, I guess." He let out a little chuckle. "So, when I was born, they named me Lesus Moore." He looked down at his half-eaten sandwich. "So there, now you know my deepest embarrassment."

"I've been married six times," I blurted out. "Now you know mine."

He looked up at me and at first, I thought he thought I was kidding. "Really?" he asked.

"Really. I don't ever tell anyone that so don't go blabbing it around town. Actually, I'd prefer it if you kept that little tidbit to yourself." Why did I just share that with him? I definitely didn't want that to get around.

"I won't tell a soul," he said, and I believed him. "Since we're sharing secrets, I'll tell you what's in my notebook."

I sat up straight. Finally!

He reached over and pushed it toward me. "Don't laugh," he said and I promised I wouldn't. "I write poetry." His face flushed a little. "I'm not like my parents. They love the spotlight and both love to entertain. I'm…quieter. But I like writing because I can put down all of my emotions and observations. It's kind of a like a conversation with myself."

"May I?" I asked, glancing at the notebook.

"Sure," he said, nervously removing his hand from the cover.

I opened it up to the middle and started reading aloud quietly.

In A Tree

Does she see me,
Do I dare.
Does she notice,
When I stare.
In the branches,
End of day.
She turned the lights out,
I sneak away.

LES GRABBED the notebook from me, his face so red it was nearly purple. "Uhhh, forget that one," he stammered. "Read a different one."

He flipped through the notebook and handed it back to me. "Try this one."

I narrowed my eyes at him while I took the notebook. This one had better be a little less stalkerish.

Too Soon

I saw you today, laying on the sidewalk,
Once so full of life, dancing in the wind.
Oh so green, so tall, so straight,
Never to break, only slightly bend.
I knelt down, and picked you up,

Brown and brittle.
Cut too soon from this life,
Oh blade of grass, you were so little.

I LAUGHED. "OKAY," I admitted. "That one's cute."

He smiled. "I like to write about everyday objects. The things that are truly amazing but everyone takes for granted or just ignores."

I had a feeling he was talking more about himself than grass at that moment.

"So, do you go to, like, poetry readings or anything? Some place to read your poetry in public?"

"Oh no!" he chuckled as he took the notebook away from me. "That's not really my thing."

"Well, I think you should!" I encouraged. "Your poetry is really good."

He shrugged. "Maybe one day. I'd really like to get my poems published. That's kind of my dream."

"Well, there you go!" I said excitedly. "So, you know what you want to do with your life after all!"

He smiled. "Yeah, I guess I do."

We took another bite of our sandwiches and I tried to figure out how to ask him about the condos. He really didn't seem like the kind of guy that would have the funds to do that kind of thing.

"So," I said, still not sure how I was going to word this. "After my grandma and I get our new store up and

SHANNON VANBERGEN

running, we were thinking about getting into the condo business. Maybe building some on the edge of town."

"Really?" he asked, surprised. "I've only met her a few times, but she doesn't seem like the kind of person who would do that?"

"What do you mean?" I asked.

"Well," he said, worried that he offended me. "I don't mean anything bad by it. Just that I thought that was something investors did. Ya know, people with a lot of money to spend...or risk."

"My grandmother has plenty of money to spend." Now I *was* offended.

"No, I didn't mean it like that. I guess I just picture mysterious people who live far away from here who pay someone else to scope out the area but they never actually visit themselves. But that's probably just my imagination getting the best of me again."

Actually, that was how I pictured it too.

"So, you would never build a condo?" I asked.

"Oh no. That's not my thing at all."

Hmmm. Either he was lying or the Grannies were mistaken.

I dropped the subject and we finished our lunch, talking about our childhoods and our parents. He was surprisingly easy to talk to and it felt good to have a conversation with him. I had talked to Joe plenty of times, but we never really talked about anything deep like Les and I did.

82

My phone vibrated in my pocket and I pulled it out. Grandma Dean sent me a text and said she would be by the shop to get me in about an hour.

"I hate to cut our lunch short," I said to Les. "But my grandma is going to pick me up in an hour and I still have work to do."

"Cut it short?" He laughed. "We've been sitting here for nearly two hours!"

I looked around and was surprised to see that we were one of the few people still in the restaurant. "Wow!" I said, pushing my chair back to get up. "Time flies when you're having fun!"

"I had fun too," he said sheepishly. "Maybe we could do this again?"

"I would love to! And maybe you'll let me read some more of your poetry."

"It's a date!" he said, then quickly backtracked. "I mean, it's a..."

"That's alright, Les," I said, clapping him on the back. "I know what you mean."

When we left the shop, I went my way and Les went his. I couldn't help but think about what he said about the condo. Why would he lie about something like that? He shared all kinds of things with me at lunch, so why not that? I wanted to talk to someone about it but I knew I couldn't talk to Grandma Dean. She didn't think he could ever do anything wrong, and honestly, I didn't either. But this really bothered me. Then it dawned on me. If there was one granny I could talk to about this, it was Greta. She seemed to be on my side about Les from the beginning. Now if I could just get her alone to talk to her. That might be more difficult than it was to get information out of Les. But I had to try. Stan's life might depend on it.

CHAPTER 10

When Grandma Dean picked me up a little over an hour later, she was clearly irritated.

"Would you believe the police aren't going to put Stan in any kind of witness protection program? Someone tried to kill him and they are just sending him back home!"

"Really?" I asked with surprise. "They aren't even putting an officer on him?"

"Well," Grandma said, turning toward the retirement community. "They said they would do that, but the poor guy is terrified to go home. Plus, his window isn't even fixed yet. So, yet again, we had to take things into our own hands."

Uh oh.

"What does that mean?" I asked.

"He's going to be staying with Hattie until we solve this. That way he won't be alone."

"Hattie?" I burst out laughing. "Well, who's going to save him from her?!"

"What does that mean?" Grandma asked.

"First of all," I pointed out, "I think Hattie has the hots for him. Secondly, she's a nutcase! Out of all the Grannies, why would you let him stay with her?"

"I'm not so sure she has the hots for him," Grandma corrected. "I think she's just lonely. And she was the first one to say he could stay with her. What was I supposed to do?"

I shrugged.

"What's done is done," Grandma said, pulling into the parking lot of the retirement village. "We're meeting at Hattie's house. Everyone is already there. Do you want to come with me?"

I was honored to be invited. I thought my date with Larry had really proved my worth to the group—or at least the depths I would go to for them.

When we walked into Hattie's house, I was instantly taken back by how hot it was. Grandma must have seen my reaction because she leaned toward me and whispered, "Hattie keeps her thermostat set to 'Hell.' Make sure you drink plenty of water so you don't dehydrate."

The Grannies were already sitting at the table with their tall glasses of ice water. Grandma snuck into the hallway to turn on the air so no one passed out from a heatstroke.

Hattie's apartment had the same layout as Grandma

Dean's, but hers was decorated very differently. Grandma's style was very modern while Hattie's was more...seventies. The walls were a pale yellow, either from paint or from time, and the accents of avocado green and burnt orange dated the place even further. But still, it had a cozy, lived-in feel that was comforting.

From my place at the table, I could see Stan, sitting quietly, lost in his thoughts in a beat-up recliner in the living room.

"Stan," Virginia said to him. "Would you like to come in here and sit with us so we can talk to you?"

He shook his head no. "The killer might see me through that window." He pointed toward the large kitchen window next to the table. "I think I'm safer in here."

"There's a policeman right outside the door," Grandma assured him as she emerged from the hallway. "I think you'll be safe."

Stan clearly wasn't budging.

"We'll just sit in the living room," Hattie said, getting up and walking in there. All the Grannies followed her and took a seat either on the couch or the loveseat. There wasn't any room left so I sat on the floor.

Grandma filled him in on her epiphany from the night before. "Stan, we got to talking about things after..." She motioned toward his arm, not wanting to say the word "shooting" and get him all upset. "And we think we came up with something. What if Artie wasn't the target this whole time…but you were?"

She let her words sink in before she continued. He sat there motionless and speechless.

"I'm going to ask you some questions that might make you uncomfortable, but if you can answer honestly, we might be able to help you."

Stan looked up at Grandma Dean, a grave look on his face. "You think he died…because of me?"

"We aren't sure," Virginia said gently. "It's just a theory right now."

Stan shook his head. "I'll tell you anything you want to know."

Grandma didn't waste any time with the questioning. "Did you owe anyone money?"

Stan shook his head no.

"Do you have any kids that might be upset with you and that might benefit from your will?"

He shook his head again.

"What about any jilted lovers?"

The other Grannies flashed Grandma Dean a dirty look. "What?" she asked them. "We have to ask."

"Actually," Stan said to the surprise of everyone. "I do have someone…"

In the nearly two years they had known Stan, he had never once mentioned a woman in his life. They all knew he had been married but assumed his wife had died years ago. The Grannies leaned forward, anxious to hear his story.

"I married a woman a few years ago. She was a bit younger than me. Everyone told me she just married me for my money. We were only together a short while until she up and moved out. We were never actually divorced, though."

"Oh my gosh!" Hattie exclaimed. "I'm living with a married man?" She looked down at me and winked and mouthed the words, "That's so hot!"

I rolled my eyes. We really needed to get Stan out of here. He was either going to suffocate from the heat or from Hattie being *in* heat.

"Do you think maybe she hired someone to come after you? Knock you off so she gets your money?" Irene asked.

"I don't know." Stan looked at each of us. "I don't know anything anymore. She didn't seem like the kind of person who would do that. But I haven't seen her in a while. Eventually, I sold our house and moved in here. I was tired of being lonely. I don't know what kind of person she turned into."

"Maybe she's in need of money," Virginia said. "Maybe she's desperate."

"Money will make you do crazy things," Greta added. "It's the root of all evil, if you ask me."

We sat there quietly for a minute, thinking things over. Finally, Grandma stood up.

"What's her name?" Grandma asked. "We'll go find her and find out if she's behind this or not."

"Sydnie Bennet," he replied gently, a small smile

appearing on his face. It was obvious that he still cared for her.

"We'll find her and get to the bottom of this," Grandma reassured him. "Do you have any idea where she might have moved to?"

"I hired a PI to find her not long after she left. He said she was in Fairhope, AL. I don't know if she's still there or not." Stan looked up at Grandma with pleading eyes. "Make sure nothing bad happens to her."

"I will," Grandma said. "But if she's guilty of this, you know she'll have to deal with the consequences.

"I know," he said quietly. "I know."

CHAPTER 11

WITH A NAME AND A LAST KNOWN LOCATION, WE WERE out the door and on our way back to Grandma's apartment not far from Hattie's. I was disappointed that I didn't have a chance to talk to Greta about Les, but I knew it hadn't been the right time. I didn't want Grandma Dean to know what I was up to.

We weren't home twenty minutes when Grandma walked excitedly into my room. "I found her!" she exclaimed. "She's still in Fairhope and I have an address. Do you want to come along on a road trip?"

"You're driving there?" I asked, surprised.

"Well, of course! This should be fun. I think I'll invite Greta and Virginia and leave Irene here to keep an eye on Stan and Hattie. She doesn't really like to travel anyway."

"But why don't you just *call* Stan's wife? That would be so much faster...and easier."

"Nikki, you can't always take the easy route in life! Where's the fun in that? Besides, if she really is behind all of this, I think she's more apt to talk to us if we're standing at her front door then just hiding behind a receiver."

Grandma smiled and nudged me on the shoulder. "You live like you're an old lady! You have plenty of years to just sit around. Come on this adventure with me!"

A road trip did sound like fun. And I liked everyone Grandma was inviting. Not that I didn't like Irene and Hattie, Virginia and Greta just seemed a little more down to earth. And nicer to me.

"Alright," I said with a sigh.

Grandma Dean clapped her hands in front of her. "Great! I'll call Greta and Virginia! We'll leave in the morning! It's a nearly ten-hour drive and I'm hoping to stop as little as possible."

Um, that definitely didn't sound like fun.

I found out that "stopping as little as possible" still meant stopping every two hours. Apparently, granny bladders were extremely tiny and it didn't help that we had to stop at every *Cracker Barrel* along the way. But I had to admit, it really was fun.

I had come to Florida just a few months ago and it was my first time out of Illinois. Since I flew, I didn't get to see anything exciting. Of course, having sat in a car for hours upon hours from Peace Pointe, FL to Fairhope, I didn't see too many exciting things either.

But the view was beautiful and the stories the Grannies told were entertaining.

About halfway there, our conversations turned to Stan and his mysterious wife.

"I wonder why she left him," Virginia said from the backseat next to me. "Stan is such a nice guy."

"Who knows," Grandma Dean said, switching lanes. "You never know what goes on behind closed doors. He could be a completely different husband than he is a friend."

We sat there quietly for a moment and I assumed we were all thinking over Grandma's words. I glanced over at Virginia, who was looking out her window. I wondered what had happened to her husband...and Greta's too. They both had kids, so that meant there had to be a Mr. Virginia and Mr. Greta at some point.

"What about your husband?" I asked Virginia quietly. "What happened to him?"

Virginia looked at me in surprise. I was new to the group and I didn't really know much about any of the Grannies. I also didn't know what was okay to ask about and what wasn't. The look she gave me made me think I had wandered into the "what not to ask" category, but then her face softened.

"Frank and I were married for twenty years...and then he left me for his secretary." Virginia laughed when she saw the look on my face. "It's okay," she said, patting my arm. "It ended up being for the best."

"How was it for the best?" I asked. I could still see hurt in her eyes, hiding behind her smile.

"She went on to meet Raul!" Greta laughed. "Tell Nikki about him!"

Virginia's face flushed. "There isn't much to say!"

Greta snorted and Virginia laughed too. "We met on a mission trip to Haiti," Virginia finally continued. "I was a nurse and went over there to help out for a few weeks. Raul was from Philadelphia. We hit it off right away."

"Did you date him?" I asked. Virginia was a beautiful woman in her seventies. I couldn't imagine how stunning she must have been in her forties. But it was still hard for me to imagine any of the Grannies having a love life.

"They ran away together!" Greta jumped in. "Can you imagine that! Our good little Virginia ran away with a man and traveled the world!"

Virginia laughed. "We didn't really travel the world. We went to a few countries together, just two nurses who had a heart for people."

"And for each other." Greta leaned over her shoulder from the front seat and winked at her.

"So, what happened to Raul?" I asked.

Virginia sighed. "After two years, the spark died out. We looked at each other one day and realized we were two lonely people in a foreign country trying to put some meaning into our meaningless little lives." She shook her head, "The funny thing is, the day before, we were two exciting lovers on a course to change the world. It's crazy how quickly things can change."

"Must have been something you ate," Greta said, still facing us. "I heard foreign food will do that to you."

Virginia laughed. "Maybe it was."

"What about you?" I asked Greta. "What about your husband?"

The car was quiet. I had definitely gone into the "what not to ask" category this time.

"It's complicated," she said, turning back to the front seat.

"You don't have to talk about it," Grandma said to her, reaching over and putting a hand on her arm.

I felt bad. This was obviously a part of Greta's life that still caused her pain. I tried to think of what I could talk about instead. Maybe bring up my own failures? That was definitely a lengthy list that would get us almost all the way to Alabama.

"I was married for forty years," Greta said, to my surprise. "Forty long years to a man who only knew I existed if I didn't have dinner on the table at the same time every night. And for the most part, I tolerated it. I had my house and my kids, my charities, my church. I had enough in my life that brought me joy. I didn't need a husband for that. But one day, I snapped."

Uh oh. Was this the part in her story where she says she chopped off his head and fed it to the neighbor's dog? I cringed, waiting for a gruesome story to unfold and then to be threatened with my life if I told a single soul.

"It was my sixtieth birthday and do you know what he did on that day? He went golfing with his friends! All day! He came home that evening, walked in the door and said, 'What's for dinner?' I stood there in my dress, my hair all done and my makeup on, and I smiled at him and reminded him that it was my birthday. He looked right at me and said, 'Well, we still hafta eat so what are you cookin?'" Greta was quiet for a minute. "Normally, I would've gone into the kitchen and made him dinner, crying quietly here and there and trying to thank the Good Lord for my nice house, children, and grandchildren—trying to count each and every blessing. But not that time."

Oh dear, here it comes.

"Instead, something snapped. My good heart pulled up anchor and I stood up tall and told him to make his own darn dinner. I went in our room, packed up my things, and knew then I was never coming back."

I hated to admit it, but her story was kind of a letdown. I was expecting much worse. I clearly read too many mystery novels.

"When I came back in the living room, he just glared at me," Greta sniffled a little. "I held my head high and tried to walk past him. He tensed his shoulders and puffed out his chest, and brought his elbows out just enough that they hit me when I walked by him. It was the first time he ever physically did anything to show force and I wanted to make sure it was the last. I glanced down and saw the mail sitting on the table in the entryway. Without thinking, I picked up the letter opener and stabbed him in the neck."

I gasped. After the initial letdown, I didn't see that coming!

"It was a sharp little thing and it caused a lot of blood, but thankfully, it wasn't anything serious. I heard later he got a stitch or two, but he never called the police. Instead, he let me walk out of his life. That was over fifteen years ago and we haven't talked since."

"You did what you had to do," Virginia said. "In my opinion, he's lucky that's all that happened to him."

Greta pulled a tissue from her purse and dabbed at her eyes. "I'm not proud of it. And even though the kids have never brought it up to me, I feel like they know what happened. Every time I go up there to visit for the holidays, they make sure to have a meal with me and a separate one with him. Maybe they're afraid I'll stab him with a fork or something."

"Well, as sad as that is," Virginia said, "I think Geraldine still holds the title of saddest breakup."

Grandma shifted uncomfortably in the driver's seat. I could see her face go red, but Greta and Virginia didn't seem to notice.

"I agree," Greta said sadly. "Breaks my heart every time I think about it."

Since Grandpa Glenn had died several years ago and they had a wonderful marriage, as far as I could tell anyway, I knew they weren't talking about him. She had met him when she was nineteen. He was her agent and they fell in love instantly. When they met, my grandmother had a daughter, my mother, with another man. When my mother was just eighteen months old, Grandma Dean left her with her own mother so she could start her acting career in Europe. Greta and Virginia must have been talking about my mother's father. Grandma has always been tightlipped about him and, other than seeing a picture that fell out of a photo album that could possibly be him, no one in my family knew anything about him. I held my breath, waiting, hoping, that maybe she would share the story.

"That's a story for another time," she said sternly. Greta and Virginia turned to look at her and then Virginia glanced over at me. "Of course," she said, concerned. "I don't know what I was thinking. I'm sorry I brought it up."

Grandma shrugged and let out a forced laugh. "Enough about all of these depressing matters! Let's talk about something fun!"

We each tried to bring up a lighthearted topic, but each one quickly fizzled out. It wasn't long before we heard Greta snoring, so we all settled into our own quiet thoughts as we watched the fields fly by in a blur.

CHAPTER 12

SINCE WE PULLED IN AT NIGHT, I DIDN'T GET A GOOD look at the town. But now that it was morning, I could see that it was the most charming town I had ever seen. Our bed and breakfast gave us a view of Mobile Bay and the sight was breathtaking.

The morning air was humid as we headed out, our bellies full of the delicious homemade breakfast the owners had made for us. I had a thought that maybe once I got my life together and left Grandma Dean's apartment, maybe I would just move here instead of going back to Illinois. There was something about that little town that just felt...special. It was the kind of place Les Moore would love. He could write a million poems here and still not run out of things to write about. I'd have to tell him about it.

That last thought raced back through my mind. Was I actually looking forward to talking to him again? I inwardly scolded myself. Les seemed like a nice guy—not the kind I would want to end up in my "web" as Irene had put it. But still, even if I didn't pursue things romantically, he could still be a good friend. Of course, I had to find out first what was up with that condo thing.

We drove through the cutest little downtown area I had ever seen. Flowers lined the street, sat in bunches at the corners, and hung from lamp posts. An old-timey-looking clock sat in the middle of a brick sidewalk, giving the downtown charm and character.

Virginia kept driving, following the directions of the GPS, and we ended up in a little neighborhood. Small, unassuming houses sat close to the street, their yards littered with children's toys. We pulled in front of a gray one-story with a little white porch. The yard, though toy-free, was unkempt and the bushes were tall enough to nearly block the entire large, front window.

"This is it," Virginia said, turning off the vehicle. "You gals ready?"

We took a collective deep breath and unbuckled our seatbelts. "Let's do this," Grandma Dean said, grabbing her purse.

We walked up the creaky steps with Grandma leading the way and me bringing up the rear. Grandma knocked on the door and we waited. We didn't hear any sounds from the inside and were about to turn and leave when we saw movement through the small window in the door.

A young blond woman, who looked to be in her early twenties, opened the door. "Hello," she said with a big smile. "Can I help you?"

We froze for a second, surprised to see someone so young at the door. We knew then that Stan was going to be in for a big surprise. "Hello," Grandma finally said. "Is your mother here?"

The girl's face dropped. "I'm sorry," she said. "She died several years ago. She had a brain aneurism."

"Oh my," Greta said. "I'm so sorry."

The girl looked at us a little confused. "Were you friends of hers?"

We looked at each other, not sure what to say. This was not how we thought this visit was going to go.

"We knew her a little," Grandma lied. "We just thought we'd come for a little visit."

The girl gave us a perplexed look. "Where are my manners," she said, the smile returning to her face. "Would you like to come in?"

"Oh no," Grandma said. "We don't want to impose. We should get going anyway."

We turned and walked back to the car, leaving the bewildered girl in her doorway. Once we got inside the SUV, she finally went back inside and closed her door.

"How do you think Stan is going to take the news that he has a daughter?" Grandma asked.

"I don't know," Greta said. "But when you call him, put him on speaker so we can all hear!"

Grandma dialed his number and he answered right away, his voice laced with worry.

"Stan," Grandma said to him. "We have some news."

"Okaaaay," Stan said slowly. "What is it?"

"Well," Grandma said. "I hate to tell you this, but Sydnie...has passed. She had a brain aneurism a few years ago."

"Oh my gosh," Stan said. This was obviously devastating news. "It runs in her family. I just can't believe it though." His voice cracked.

"But," Grandma continues. "That means she isn't the one who either tried to kill you or hired someone to kill you."

Stan was silent on the other end except for a muffled sob.

"We have more news," Grandma said, taking a deep breath. "And this one is a doozy."

"What is it?" Stan sniffed.

"You're a father."

We all held our breaths as we waited for his reaction.

"What?" he asked, shocked. "Are you sure?"

"Yes," Grandma confirmed.

"And she's really nice," Greta yelled from the backseat. "And very pretty."

"Where is she?" Stan asked, almost panicked. "Who's she staying with?"

"She lives by herself as far as we can tell," Grandma answered.

"What?" Stan screamed into the phone.

"It's okay," Grandma said quickly. "She looked healthy…"

"Get back over there!" he demanded. "And bring her back with you!"

"Stan," Grandma tried to comfort him. "She's doing okay…"

Stan cut her off. "So help me, Geraldine, if you don't go in there and get her, I'll drive over there and get her myself."

We all looked at each other, shocked with the tone he had taken with Grandma.

"Okay," Grandma finally said. "I'll see what I can do."

Grandma got off the phone and we looked at each other. "What in the heck was that all about?" Virginia asked.

Greta sighed. "People don't think millennials can take care of themselves. I hear about it all the time on the news. Stan's only known he was a father for five minutes and already he's a helicopter parent."

We got out of the vehicle and started the familiar walk back up the girl's porch. We all stepped back and let Grandma Dean be the one to handle things. "Thanks," she said to us sarcastically.

Grandma knocked on the door and the girl answered right away this time. Most likely she had been watching us from the window, wondering what

SHANNON VANBERGEN

in the heck we were doing loitering in front of her house.

She smiled at us like she did before, but there was a hint of wariness behind it. "Hello again," she said brightly.

"Hello," Grandma said nervously. "We were wondering if we could talk to you again for a minute."

"About my mother?" she asked.

"No," Grandma said slowly. "Do you know someone named Stan Bennet?"

"Stan?" she asked, clearly concerned. "Is he okay?"

"So, you know about him?"

"Of course," she said, moving aside. "Please, come in."

We walked straight into her living room, which was dark thanks to the overgrown bush outside the window. She motioned for us to sit down on the overly worn furniture. We all took a seat and she sat down in a chair near the kitchen. From where I sat, I could see my reflection in the old box television that sat across the room.

"Is Stan okay?" she asked again.

"Well," Grandma started. "I hate to tell you this, but it seems someone is after him."

"What do you mean?" she asked, her eyes as big as the coffee stains on the furniture.

"Someone is trying to kill him," Greta blurted out.

The girl was shocked and put her hand to her mouth. "Is he okay?"

"He's okay for now," Grandma assured her. "But he's worried about you. He...wants you to come back to Florida with us."

The girl's eyes started to fill with tears. "He wants me to come to Florida? To see him?"

Grandma nodded.

I could tell we were all trying to figure out the same thing—were those happy tears or sad tears?

Suddenly, she bolted upright. "Give me a minute to pack my things! Can I ride with you? There's no way my car will make it that far!"

We all looked at each other, not expecting this turn of events. Finally, Grandma nodded. With that, the girl ran out of the room and disappeared into a hallway off the living room.

"Looks like we'll be adding another passenger to the ride home," Grandma said unenthusiastically. "I guess that gives us plenty of time to get to know her."

"I'm sure she'll have plenty of questions about Stan," Virginia said, brushing crumbs off the couch next to her. She sighed. "Poor girl. At least her mother told her a little bit about him, or at least his name."

It wasn't long before the girl came back in the living room carrying two suitcases. "Do you think you'll have room for my things?" she asked.

"Oh yes," Virginia assured her. "We have plenty of room."

"Great!" she said happily. "I'll be right back." She disappeared down the hall again.

Greta laughed. "Maybe you should've asked how much more she had before you answered that question."

We all stood and Greta and I grabbed her two suitcases since we were sitting the closest to them. We could hear her coming back down the hall and Virginia stepped forward to help her with whatever baggage she had this time. But when she appeared, we all froze. That wasn't the baggage we expected her to be carrying.

When she saw our faces, she froze too. "Stan's going to hate me, isn't he?" she asked, tears filling her eyes again.

We stood there, speechless, not sure what was going on. "I know I should've told him. And now you're all staring at me, judging me." She started to cry.

We looked at each other, unsure what to say. "Stan could never hate you," Grandma said, putting her arm around the girl. The half-awake toddler in her arms started to cry too.

"There, there," Greta said, rushing toward the child. "It's okay."

"This is Stan's…" Grandma stopped, hoping the girl would fill in the blank.

"Daughter," the girl finally said.

Oh my gosh! Boy, did we have it all wrong!

"Are you Sydnie?" Virginia asked.

"Well, of course," she said, sniffling. "Who did you

think I was? Oh my goodness. Did you think *I* was his daughter?"

"No," we said at once. But Grandma turned and grimaced. Hopefully the girl, Sydnie, didn't see right through us.

"So, who is this precious little one?" Greta asked, touching the little girl's hair.

"This is Lillian Rose Bennet," Sydnie said proudly. "But I call her Lily."

A chorus of "aww" rang out from the Grannies and I was pushed aside as they all went up to her to baby-talk their approval.

Standing back and taking a good look at Lily, I could tell she was related to Stan. She had his gray-blue eyes and the same dimple in her chin.

"Can one of you hold her?" Sydnie asked. "I need to pack her some snacks, if that's okay."

"I'll take her," Virginia said the quickest. I could hear Greta let out a sigh of disappointment.

Grandma turned to her and whispered, "Greta, why don't you run outside really quick and call Stan. Let him know we were mistaken."

Grandma was pushing the job off on Greta but she didn't seem to mind. "I'll come with you," I said, following her out the door.

She had already dialed Stan's number by the time we made it down the porch steps. Stan answered, his voice still full of panic.

"Stan," Greta said, a nervous excitement to her voice. "I'm calling with some more news."

"Is the child okay?" I could clearly hear his voice, even though the phone was pressed to Greta's ear.

"Yes," she said, looking up at me. "And she's coming home with us." Greta put her hand over the phone and whispered to me, "Let's not tell him the whole story." I nodded in agreement.

I couldn't tell exactly what he was saying but he sounded relieved. "And there's more news," she said. "It turns out we were wrong. Her mother, Sydnie, is still alive."

He said something that I couldn't make out and Greta let out nervous laughter. "Yeah," she said. "It was just a misunderstanding."

Stan's words were muffled again and Greta answered him. "Yes, we'll see you tomorrow. I'll take a picture of her and text it to you when we get in the car." She was quiet for a minute. "She's a beautiful little girl, Stan. She looks just like you."

When Greta got off the phone, she had tears in her eyes. "I've never heard him so happy," she said, wiping away a tear that had escaped and ran down her cheek. "We got to tell a very sad man today that he is a father. What a crazy, unexpected day this has been."

She turned to walk up to the house and I remembered that I needed to talk to her. "Greta," I said, reaching out and touching her arm. "Can I ask you something really quick?"

THE ROOT OF ALL EVIL

"Of course," she said, stopping on the sidewalk.

"You said the other night that you saw an unsigned contract with Les's name on it at Larry's house, right?"

"I did," Greta confirmed.

"Are you sure it had his name on it? Was it maybe a different Les?"

"No, it was him," Greta said. "I even took a picture of it to show you." She pulled out her phone and looked through her pictures. "Here," she said, handing it to me.

Sure enough, in the middle of the picture was the contract. As I studied it, something else got my attention. Behind it, partially covered by Les's contract, was another contract with the exact same information but with a different name—William Conrady. *That's weird*, I thought. Why would there be two contracts for the exact same property with different names on them?

Before I had time to come up with an answer, Grandma and Virginia came out of the house carrying suitcases with Sydnie carrying her daughter and a large baby bag.

Within minutes, we were all buckled in the SUV and I had been sequestered to the third row so Greta could sit in the middle with Sydnie and Lily. Since Lily's carseat was rear-facing—Sydnie said it was safer that way—I got a good view of the little girl. She still looked half-asleep, but even so, she smiled and laughed as Greta played peek-a-boo with her.

"May I take a picture of her?" Greta asked Sydnie. "To show Stan? I promised him I would."

"Sure," Sydnie said. She leaned in close to her daughter and Greta took a picture of them both. Before Greta sent the picture, I saw the text. "Your wife and daughter are coming home."

Suddenly, a man who had no people had a family.

CHAPTER 13

THE RIDE BACK TO PEACE POINTE WENT AS SMOOTHLY AS it could with a vehicle full of grandmas and a toddler. We had taken turns driving and sitting next to Lily. I had never really wanted kids, but I had to admit, she was adorable.

We perfectly retraced our route home, clear down to the bathroom and *Cracker Barrel* stops. In between each one, we got to know a little more about Sydnie and even a little bit about Stan.

"So how did you two meet?" Virginia asked.

Sydnie cringed. "I'm afraid it isn't a very exciting story."

"Oh, tell it anyway," Greta urged.

"Well," she started. "I dropped out of college because it just wasn't my thing and I got a job with a local theater group. The pay was lousy—just tips—but we had so much fun. One day, we were performing some comedy in the park and this old guy kept staring at me and laughing. At the end, he was literally bent over he was laughing so hard! I went over to him to tell him how much it meant to me that he enjoyed the show so much. Turns out he was actually choking! I did the Heimlich maneuver and finally, he spit out his popcorn. He thanked me and said he had been choking like that for the longest time! I felt so bad!"

"Oh my goodness!" Virginia exclaimed. "He could've died!"

"I know, right?" Sydnie laughed. "It was the funniest thing! He was shaking pretty bad so I offered to buy him a coffee or something. We walked to the coffee shop across the street from the park and we just started talking. You know Stan, he's super nice. I told him how I was struggling financially and he offered me his guest house. Well, I could barely pass that up! Soon he was taking me to dinners and buying me clothes. It's not like he had anyone else to spend money on. He had been married before but his wife died years ago and she wasn't able to have children. I guess we just both found what we needed in each other."

Yeah, I thought. *You needed a father and he needed a child.*

Every once in a while, if you're really fortunate, you'll meet someone, and after you've talked to them for a little bit and you hear how genuine they are, you'll think to yourself, "This is a really cool person. They are really going to make a difference in this world." Sydnie was not one of those people.

It seemed like no matter how many times we asked her something, her answer always had to do with money...Stan's money. As we listened to her, we started to regret bringing her back with us. I felt a tenseness in the air as one by one, the Grannies stopped talking to her and tried to act like they were dozing off. But that didn't stop Sydnie from talking.

"Did you know that Stan went to a community college?" she asked us after several long, silent minutes. "Can you believe he made a fortune with just an associate's degree? I guess that's why I fell in love with him."

Because he made a fortune? I wanted to say.

"If you loved him, why did you leave him?" Greta asked, her voice a little terse.

"People grow apart," Sydnie said sadly. "I lived in his guest house for three months and then we were married. We lasted a year, though. After that, I started to feel like he was winding down his life and I was just starting mine. It was just a weird combination. So," she said with a deep breath, "I packed up late one night and took off with his Cadillac and some cash. I'm not proud of it, but that's what I did. A few weeks later, I found out I was pregnant."

I thought we all wanted to ask her why she didn't tell Stan about Lily, but none of us asked her because we just couldn't take another one of her selfish answers.

It was late when we pulled up in front of the retirement community. Lily was sound asleep in her car seat, holding Greta's hand. "I hate to let go," she whispered to Sydnie. Greta was definitely the most grandma-ish one in the group. Virginia was a close second.

We piled out of the SUV, trying to be quiet so we wouldn't wake Lily.

"You two can stay at my place tonight," Greta offered. "Then we can take you to see Stan in the morning."

Sydnie agreed and we helped carry her luggage to Greta's apartment. Once she was settled in Greta's guest room, we returned to the SUV to get our own luggage.

"What have we done?" Virginia asked, shaking her head on the way back to her vehicle.

"I don't know," Grandma Dean said with a sigh. "But I don't like this one bit."

I SLEPT in the next morning, exhausted from our little trip. Grandma Dean came in around nine and asked me if I wanted to head to Stan's apartment. She said Greta had just called her and said they were all on their way over there.

I declined. That was a reunion I didn't want to be a part of.

I stayed in bed a little longer until I got a text from Les, asking if I wanted to meet him at the coffee shop downtown in an hour. I jumped at the chance to get breakfast.

I barely messed with my hair, just pulled it into a pony tail. I put on a thin layer of mascara and slid on some lip gloss—two things I never would've done had Grandma Dean not started to have an influence on me.

An hour later, I was sitting at a table, sipping a vanilla bean frappe. A huge cinnamon bun dripping with caramel sauce sat in front of me, waiting to be devoured. Somehow I had managed to beat Les there, but I was okay with that. I enjoyed the few quiet minutes when it was just me and my pastry.

As I stared at it, praying for the forgiveness of the gluttonous crime I was about to commit, Les sat at the table. He held a coffee in one hand, a hot apple tart in the other, and his notebook tucked under his arm.

"Sorry, I'm a little late," he said, sitting down. "I had my car looked at this morning. I think it's leaking gas. The appointment took a little longer than I thought."

"No problem," I said through a mouthful of deliciousness.

Les laughed. "Is it that good?" he asked.

I rolled my eyes yes in delight.

Les cut into his apple tart. "I heard you went on a little trip."

"How do you know about that?" I asked, surprised.

He shrugged. "Small town."

Inwardly, I laughed. Most likely he had a poem in his notebook about how, from his spot in a tree, he saw me leave the house with a suitcase. That should probably have creeped me out, but for some reason, it didn't.

"We went to this cute little town called Fairhope. You would love it!"

"I've been there!" he said excitedly. "My grandparents lived about twenty miles away in Mobile and we would go to Fairhope when we visited."

I sighed. "I would love to live there. It was so charming."

"It's expensive," he sighed. "At least the housing is. My parents thought about moving there a couple of years ago, or at least having a second house so they could be close to Mammie."

"That's what you call your grandma?" I asked.

"Yeah." Les blushed. "Mammie and Pappie."

"There's nothing wrong with that. I think it's cute!"

We sat in silence for a minute, enjoying our breakfast, when Les spoke up again. "So, I didn't tell you this the other day because I didn't want you to laugh, but I'm taking a couple classes at the local community college. One of them is a writing class."

"Why would I laugh? I think that's great!" I said, encouraging him. "Like poetry?"

"Yeah, it's mostly been reading some famous poems

and going over structure and things like that. But we've worked a little bit on our own poems. The instructor said he wanted to have a little poetry reading. I was wondering if you wanted to come. It's nothing serious or anything, just something we're doing in class. It's next Wednesday at three."

"I'd love to come!" I was really proud of Les. Not only was he going to read his poetry out loud, but he felt comfortable enough to invite someone to listen to it

"What other classes are you taking?" I asked.

His cheeks turned red and he suddenly became interested in the crumbs left by the previous occupant of our table.

"Come on!" I said, leaning across the table and lightly punching him in the arm. "Tell me!"

He laughed and looked up at me. "Okay," he said. "But don't tease me too much about it."

Since I had my mouth full with another bite of my cinnamon bun, I made the "cross my heart" sign across my chest.

"Floral arranging," he finally said.

I couldn't stop my eyes from popping wide open, but I did manage to not laugh and spit my pastry all over the table.

"What made you decide to take that class?" I asked as soon as I regained my composure.

His cheeks turned red again. "I heard it was a great way to meet women."

Now I couldn't hold back my laughter. "Are you serious?" I asked. "You're taking that class to pick up chicks?"

He let out a nervous laugh. "Yeah, but everyone in there is over fifty and they all have to rush home afterward because it's an evening class and apparently older women go to bed earlier."

"I could've told you that," I laughed. I looked at him sitting across the table and was touched by how open he was being with me. "You're that lonely, huh?" I asked, fully understanding the feeling.

He shrugged. "It's hard to meet women, especially when you're a little…awkward."

"You're not awkward," I lied. "You're sweet and charming." That part was true.

Les smiled and took a sip of his coffee, then pointed to my frappe. "No coffee for you?" he asked.

"Honestly, I hate coffee," I confided. "I drink it every once in a while, but I think it tastes like dirt."

Les laughed. "If you hate it so much, why do you drink it at all?"

I shrugged. Why did I drink it?

Les seemed nervous all of a sudden and he fidgeted with his napkin. "I wrote you a poem," he finally said. "Would you like to read it?"

"Of course!" I said, moving my plate out of the way.

He fumbled with the pages in his notebook before he found what he was looking for and handed it over.

My Gem

Your beauty is like a solar eclipse,
I want to stare at you until your image is burned into
my soul.
Your hair is so wild, falling around your face.
Like autumn leaves twirling in the breeze.
Looking into your eyes is like looking into a telescope.
At millions of twinkling stars in the galaxy.
You are a precious gem that I've spent my whole life
mining for.
I want to keep you safe in a treasure box, known only
as my heart.

"Wow," I said slowly, not sure how to react.

"You don't like it." He took the notebook from me and folded the front cover back in place.

"No, I love it! It's just that…" How could I say this without hurting his feelings? "I really like you, as a friend." Wow, those were words I had never spoken before. I sat there, a little proud of myself for not jumping into the arms of any man who showed an interest. But then it hit me—why didn't I have feelings for him?

I looked over at Les, sitting across the table, his head down and his cheeks flushed in embarrassment. He was very nice to me and he was so easy to talk to. I'd married guys for less than that. In just the few times we had gotten together, I had shared more things with him than I had with anyone else. When I was around him, I felt like I was truly myself. So why wouldn't I even *consider* dating him? Suddenly, I felt confused and guilty.

Before I had a chance to say anything else, the door to the coffee shop opened and Joe walked in, followed by several of his hunky firemen friends. They were all dressed the same, dark blue pants with a tight dark blue t-shirt with the Peace Pointe fire department logo over their chest. As soon as he saw me, he came over to say hi.

"Hey!" he said as he approached our table. He leaned down and kissed me on the forehead, which I thought was strange—almost like he was marking his territory. "What are you up to?" He looked over at Les and nodded a hello. "Who's your friend?" he asked when he turned back to me.

"This is Les," I said, suddenly nervous. "We're just sitting here, chatting."

Joe acted a little strange, then he pointed to his friends. "I better get back over there. Just wanted to say hi." He looked at Les and nodded again. "Nice to meet ya, Les."

"You too," Les said quietly.

"Oh hey," Joe said before he walked away. "Are you busy tonight? I thought we could go out for dinner."

I stammered for a minute before I finally said yes.

"Great," he said, all smiles. "I'll text you later then and we can work out the details."

He walked away and Les and I sat there for a minute in awkward silence.

"So," I finally said, trying to move on from the uncomfortable moment. "Do you know what you're going to read at your poetry reading? Or are you going to write something new?"

Les didn't seem like he was in the mood to talk anymore. "I'm not sure," he finally said.

All of a sudden, Joe reappeared. He put a coffee on the table in front of me. "I know how much you love your coffee," he said, his white teeth standing out against his tan skin. "Thought I'd get you one for the road."

"Thanks," I said, pulling it close to me. "You know I can't live without it."

Joe smiled and walked to his table and I glanced toward Les. He was practically glaring at me.

"What?" I said defensively.

Les picked up his notebook and tucked it back under his arm. "I'll see you later," he said as he picked up his own coffee. Then he looked me in the eyes and his face softened. "It's okay to be yourself, you know. You're pretty great. People might just like the real you better than the fake you. I know I do."

His words stunned me and cut me deep. No one had ever called me out like that before. It was like he had looked into my eyes and saw the real me—the one that I barely even knew anymore.

The sounds of the coffee shop faded away for a minute while I sat there, feeling exposed. At that moment, I realized for the first time that I became whatever a man wanted, while the real me retreated somewhere deep inside, afraid to let others see who she really was—except when I was around Les. The sounds of the shop—the laughter, the silverware scraping against plates, the sound of chairs being slid across the floor to accommodate another friend across the room —all came crashing back. I looked around and realized Les was gone. My eyes flickered to Joe's table and my face grew warm when I realized he had been staring at me. His face seemed twisted in concern and I felt like he was seeing me, the real me, for the first time. And I was sure he didn't like it.

CHAPTER 14

I PULLED UP IN FRONT OF GRANDMA DEAN'S APARTMENT and felt sick to my stomach after my conversation with Les. I made my way up to the door, the coffee from Joe still warm in my hand.

I pulled the top off and poured the dark liquid in the bushes, watching as it splashed onto a white flower. It soaked one of the petals and left it looking dark and wilted. I could relate.

With a deep sigh, I walked into the quiet apartment and threw my bag on the table. The curtains were still drawn in the living room, giving the space a quiet, comfortable feel. I didn't know if it was the carbs, the dark apartment or the depression, but I suddenly felt like I needed a nap.

I had just made it to the hallway when the front door flew open and five angry Grannies spilled in.

SHANNON VANBERGEN

"I'm about to have a full on come-apart!" Greta yelled, in tears.

Irene slammed the door. "You just wait until I get my hands on her! I'll wring her tiny little turkey neck!"

"What happened?" I asked, forgetting all about my own troubles.

"Wanda Turnbough is what happened!" Greta yelled, taking a tissue from Hattie. "Thank you, dear. I'm so upset. I just can't believe she would do something like that."

Virginia sat at the table and leaned across toward Greta. "She said she didn't do it," she said softly. "Maybe we should give her the benefit of the doubt."

Greta huffed. "She can't pee down my back and tell me it's raining! I know she's the one who turned me in!"

"What happened?" I repeated again, this time a little louder.

Instead of trying to answer me over the shouting, Grandma Dean walked across the room to me. "Wanda…or possibly someone else…"

"Oh," Greta seethed, "it was definitely Wanda!"

Grandma continued, "Someone turned Greta in. It's one of the rules here—no kids under eighteen are allowed to live here."

"She was just staying until she found a place of her own." Greta sobbed. "It would've been a couple of weeks at the most. Now she has to be out in twenty-four hours!"

The Grannies patted Greta's arm and tried to comfort her.

"So, what's going to happen to them?" I asked the group. "Where are Sydnie and Lily going to go?"

Virginia spoke up first. "Stan is going to rent her a house. He's putting in some calls now. I bet you she'll have a place before Lily's bedtime."

Greta sobbed again. It was becoming clear this wasn't really about Sydnie and her daughter.

"You'll be able to go over and see them whenever you want," Virginia soothed.

Greta sniffed. "I know. It was just nice to have someone else there. I don't have grandkids close by and it was so nice to have a little one running around. She even let me read her bedtime stories." Greta blew her nose. "I can't tell you the last time I had a little one in my arms."

"I know how you feel," Virginia said sadly. The Grannies became silent and my heart hurt for them. They were most likely imagining when their own children were that age, chasing them around with ease. And now here they were, seemingly forgotten. Even I had been guilty of that.

"Well," Irene said, pulling everyone out of their thoughts. "You'll always have Hattie to take care of. She's practically a child."

"It's true," Hattie said with a laugh. "I've regressed quite well. I'm not to the toddler stage yet, but I'm getting pretty close to kindergarten."

Hattie's words lightened the mood and we got a laugh at her expense, partly because it was funny and partly because it was true.

Grandma's phone buzzed. "It's Stan," she said, reading the text. "He has a house lined up for Sydnie on Harper Street. She can move in tomorrow."

We all looked at Greta, bracing ourselves for her reaction. She sniffed then shrugged a little. "At least it's a nice neighborhood."

"And it's not far from here," Virginia said brightly. "We can stop by and see the little thing whenever we want."

Greta sat up straight in her chair. "We have a lot to do then! We have to get them all set up over there. The poor things have nothing!"

The Grannies were immediately in a buzz, discussing who would give what.

"I have some old plates and silverware she can have," Hattie said, leaning toward Grandma Dean, who was writing things down. "And I might have some extra sheets and towels."

"I have some pots and pans I can give her," Greta said. "And Lily loved the quilt she slept on last night. She can have that."

Grandma went around the room and made a list of what everyone would donate. She sat back and looked it over. "That takes care of the basics. Nikki and I will run over to my antique shop in the morning and get her set up with some furniture. This will at least get her started, but you know Stan will probably be buying her all new things."

Grandma's words reminded everyone of Sydnie's intentions.

"So how did the little reunion go?" I asked. "How was Stan around Lily?"

"There wasn't a dry eye in the house," Hattie said, shaking her head. "It was the sweetest thing."

"I nearly drowned in my own tears when Sydnie walked Lily over to Stan and said, 'This is your daddy'." Virginia's eyes filled with tears just thinking about it. "The poor guy could barely get any words out."

"Well," Grandma Dean said with a sigh. "I'm glad that little family is back together, though I think we all have our concerns about Sydnie."

The Grannies nodded in agreement.

"But, that leads us back to square one with our investigation. We're not any closer to figuring out who killed Artie and who's out to get Stan than we were on the day those two walked in my door asking for help."

"I hate to be the one to bring this up again, but Greta showed me the picture she took of the contract with Les's name on it—the one you found on Larry's desk."

Grandma looked irritated. "Nikki, you need to let that go."

"You guys need to see the picture," I said firmly. "Greta, show them."

She pulled out her phone and slid her finger

SHANNON VANBERGEN

through the dozens of pictures she had already taken of Lily. "Here," she finally said, passing the phone to Grandma Dean.

At first, Grandma didn't see it, but when she did, her expression changed. "Well, that's interesting."

She passed the phone around so everyone could see the matching contract under Les's.

"Why is Edna's husband's name on that contract?" Virginia asked. "They can't afford to put up condos. She's worked at the library for years and he retired from the city at least ten years ago. I'm sure they are financially comfortable, but they wouldn't be able to put up that kind of money."

"I agree," Grandma Dean said. "Something is very suspicious about this. We need to figure out a way to talk to Larry about this without him knowing we were in his house and saw it."

A heavy knock at the door startled us all. "Who could that be?" Irene asked.

"Well, it wouldn't be Stan," Hattie said. "He's still holed up in my apartment. The poor man makes me keep the curtains drawn. It's darker than the inside of a cow at my place! And he has me check every ten minutes to make sure the policeman is still watching the door. He's about driving me nuts!"

Grandma peered through the peep hole, then turned to us and whispered, "It's Detective Owen."

The Grannies did a quick fluff of their hair and Hattie quickly applied a few coats of a deep red lipstick. She was pressing her lips together and throwing the tube back in her purse when Owen walked in.

"Good afternoon, ladies," he said sternly. "I hope I'm not interrupting anything."

"Oh no," Grandma said welcoming him in. "Can I get you a glass of sweet tea?"

"No thanks," he said, walking to the head of the table and crossing his arms. "I can't stay. I just thought I'd let you know about a conversation I just had with someone."

He eyed us all like we were children and he had just gotten a call from our principal.

"Well, spit it out," Irene quipped. "We're old ladies and you're wasting our precious time."

"Does the name Larry Kramer ring a bell to any of you?" he snapped.

We all sat up in our seats and tried not to look guilty. We were failing.

Owen went on. "He called me this morning and asked me to come out to his house. He said there had been a break-in the other night and he wrestled with whether he should report it or not because he didn't actually see anything missing. Finally, he decided it was the best thing to do."

He looked down his nose at us and we tried not to fidget in our chairs.

"I went over there and he showed me some interesting things."

He gave us a second to speak up and admit our guilt. We stayed silent. Then he pulled out a notebook and started to read from it. "Lipstick, that looks an awful lot like the one Hattie is wearing right now, was found on a wine glass."

"It's a popular color," Grandma Dean interrupted. "It's sold at every makeup counter from here to Japan."

Detective Owen smirked. "A bra, size double-D, from *Victoria Secret*."

"He's a man-whore," Irene interjected. "Any one of his tramps could've left it there."

"They could," he said with a sly smile. "But not many of them would leave it there with a gift receipt."

Our faces fell in shock. My insides started to burn and I glanced at Grandma and saw her mentally boring a hole into Hattie's head.

"We were able to trace the receipt to a credit card owned by Hattie Sue Miller. How do you explain that?"

We all looked at Hattie, too furious to speak.

"What?" Hattie said defensively. "That bra was expensive! What if he didn't like it?"

"It wasn't a gift!" Grandma snapped at her. "It was a diversion!"

Grandma sat back in her chair, disgusted.

"Whatever you *think* it was," Owen said, his tone serious again, "it was actually breaking and entering." He let his words sink in while we all squirmed in our chairs. I was pretty sure I wouldn't be hauled off to jail until Owen looked directly at me. "And don't think you're getting out of this just because you were outside. You were an accessory to a crime."

Dang it.

He was quiet long enough for all of us to picture ourselves in an orange jumpsuit until he finally spoke again. "You're lucky Larry isn't going to press charges."

We let out a collective breath of relief.

"But he does want an apology."

"We can do that," Grandma Dean spoke for the group. "And we'll make sure to thank him for being so gracious."

Detective Owen wasn't satisfied. He still had a little more lecture in him. "You ladies need to leave this investigation up to people who are actually trained and skilled to handle it. One of these days, one of you are going to get yourself killed." He narrowed his eyes at me. "Can I talk to you outside?"

I sighed. This day just kept getting better and better.

I followed him out the door while the Grannies whispered, "stay strong," as I passed them.

Once we were outside, I closed the door behind us, squinting in the bright sun. Even though the kitchen light had been turned on when the Grannies walked in earlier, it still did little to prepare me for the bright afternoon Florida sun.

"I'm really disappointed in you," Owen said to me.

"Take a number," I said under my breath.

"Do you know what kind of guy Larry is?" He didn't give me time to answer. "I don't even want to think about what could've happened to you out there in the dark with him."

"How do you know about that?" I asked, surprised.

"He showed me the video!"

The what?

"He was pretty proud of himself that he 'landed' someone like you. After he told me about the break-in, he showed me some footage from his backyard security camera. Even though it was grainy, I could still tell it was you."

That means he saw the kiss.

"Nikki, you need to be more careful. I know this guy and he's a real creep."

"I know," I said quietly.

"I have a lot of respect for your grandmother, but I'm telling you right now, if they don't stop sticking their noses where they don't belong, I'll bring them in and charge them with whatever I need to, just to keep them off the streets and safe until we figure this out."

In that moment, with his warm breath hitting my face, I believed he would too.

"Okay," I said with a sigh. "I'll go talk to them right now."

I turned to open the door to go back inside and he said my name. I turned around and saw the same look that Les had given me earlier.

"Nikki, you're better than this," he said with concern on his face.

So I'd heard.

"What did he say?" Irene asked as soon as I walked in the door.

"Oh, you know, the usual." I closed the door and sat back down in my seat with a thud. "He says he'll arrest all of you if you don't stop snooping around."

Irene rolled her eyes. "That man is like a broken record."

"Maybe he's right." My words were met with death stares. "We're not getting anywhere anyway."

"We're just not seeing things clearly," Grandma Dean insisted. "What are we missing?"

The Grannies were deep in thought when I pushed my chair back. I decided now would be a good time to disappear and get ready for my dinner with Joe. He had sent me a text and said he'd pick me up at 7:30. I wasn't sure if this was an actual date or not, but I wanted to look my best either way.

"Where are you going?" Grandma asked as I stood.

"I thought we were finished here. I was going to take a shower."

"Ohhh," Hattie said. "A shower? Right now? Someone has a hot date!"

"I don't think it's really a date," I pointed out.

"What time are you meeting?" Irene asked.

I hesitated. "Seven-thirty."

"Oh, that's definitely a date." Irene seemed awfully sure of herself.

"That's right," Hattie added. "If the guy would've

said five-thirty, then it's not a date. But anything after seven? Definitely a date."

"Sit down," Grandma said, grabbing my arm as I tried to walk by her.

"I need to get ready," I said, not wanting to hear whatever lecture I could feel coming my way.

"We need to talk first."

I glanced around the table and Grandma added, "We all have something to say."

Oh great, one more lecture to add to my day. And this would be a group effort.

"Who are you going out with?" Grandma asked.

"Joe."

Hattie fanned herself at his name. "That man is fine. Owen is fine too, but Joe is extra fine."

Irene sighed. "Detective Owen is like a finely manicured lawn. It's nice to look at but you wouldn't feel comfortable playing on it. Joe, on the other hand, now that's a yard you can play on."

"I'd like to roll around in *his* bushes!" Hattie squealed. Irene let out a laugh and gave Hattie a high-five.

Grandma rolled her eyes and put her hand on mine. "We're concerned about your…"

"Mating habits," Hattie blurted.

I cringed.

"There won't be any 'mating,'" I assured them. "We're just going out to dinner."

"Well, that's good to hear," Grandma said, patting

my hand again. "Because you came here to find yourself and we're a little concerned that you might be falling into old patterns."

I was a little offended and annoyed. "It's just dinner. But if you're all that worried, I can cancel it."

"We don't want you to cancel your plans, dear," Greta said sweetly. "We just don't want you jumping into anything."

"You're afraid I'm going to go to dinner with Joe and come back married?" I asked sarcastically.

The Grannies looked at each other.

"No," Grandma said slowly, trying to find the words to say. "We just don't want you to move things along too quickly with Joe, or any man, for that matter."

Greta leaned over the table toward me and patted my left hand, since Grandma had a firm grip on my right. "Hearts before parts. That's what my Grandmother always used to say. You have to love a man first before you…"

"I'm not going to sleep with him!" I yelled.

My forcefulness took both myself and the Grannies by surprise.

"Well, okay then." Grandma Dean let go of my hand. "I'm glad you feel that way. If you need help with your hair, let me know."

"I don't need your help," I said coldly.

I got up from the table and walked out of the kitchen and into the hall. I stood there for a minute, took a deep breath, and then walked back in.

"I'm sorry I got a little upset."

The Grannies smiled.

"It's okay," Grandma assured me. "We just care about you."

"And I appreciate that," I said, honestly.

I walked back out knowing Grandma Dean could see right through me. She knew my weaknesses about as well as I did. I might be able to fool the others, but there was no hiding the truth from her. I would totally need help with my hair.

CHAPTER 15

JOE ARRIVED AT GRANDMA DEAN'S HOUSE AT 7:20. I WAS in the bathroom applying the mandatory lip gloss when Grandma opened the door for him.

"Hey, Joe," I heard her say. "You look very handsome tonight."

I could hear Joe laugh and say thank you. I gave myself one more glance in the mirror. Kitty Purry sat on the counter looking at my reflection. "What do you think?" I asked her. "Too much eyeshadow?" She purred and I wished at that moment, Grandma Dean was in there to translate. She always seemed to know what her cats said.

Grandma Dean had performed another miracle on my hair. Why couldn't it look this amazing when I styled it? We had left it curly and there wasn't a frizz in sight. Against her wishes, I went with a pair of a jeans and a flowing top instead of a dress. She let me borrow a pair of her red flats and I actually felt pretty comfortable…until I walked out and saw Joe all dressed up. Grandma flashed me a quick "I told you so" look.

Joe saw my expression and my jeans right away. "Oh man," he said, looking sorry. "I should've told you. I made reservations for us at *Romano's*."

Since I was still pretty new to town, I didn't know what that was. I looked at Grandma Dean and she mouthed the word "fancy."

"No problem," I said with a smile that I felt I was forcing. "I'll change and be right out."

"Are you sure?" Joe asked. "We can go somewhere else."

"Nikki will be ready in just a minute," Grandma said, taking my arm. "Just make yourself at home."

As she led me to her bathroom, we passed Kitty Purry in the hall. "We still have work to do," Grandma said to her. "Let's go!"

The cat followed us back to her bathroom and I marveled at how much animals could understand.

"Okay," Grandma said with her hands on her hips. "I'm going to make a suggestion and I just want you to hear me out."

Uh oh.

"I think you should wear your new black dress."

"No way," I protested. "I want to burn that thing! I had to kiss Larry Kramer in that dress!"

"I know, I know," Grandma said, shaking her head. "And I'm sorry about that. But it looks perfect on you.

And those shoes you wore with it! They made your calves look amazing."

She was right. They really did. I sighed and said okay. The dress was brought to me and Kitty Purry and Grandma Dean waited outside the bathroom door while I put on the dress and shoes. When I opened the door a few minutes later, Grandma gasped. "You look stunning!"

Kitty Purry meowed and Grandma looked from her to me, then nodded. "Yes, I agree. Kitty says you need a smoky eye now. Sit down and I'll do it really quick." Within minutes, my eyes were smoky (and a little itchy), but Grandma still shook her head, not quite satisfied. "You're going to an Italian restaurant with an Italian," she said seriously. "How much do you want to impress Joe?"

"Umm, I don't know," I said honestly. If I said I'd really like to impress him, I was afraid I'd get the "hearts before parts" lecture again. But if I said I didn't want to impress him, I was sure I'd get a lecture on how I should always look my best. I figured I'd go with the safest answer. "What are you thinking?"

"I think you need bigger hair."

"Bigger hair?" I practically yelled. "Are you crazy?"

"He's originally from New Jersey," she said, like that should tell me all I needed to know.

I sighed. "Do whatever you want."

She carefully teased and spritzed and sprayed. When she was finished, I looked in the mirror. It looked more like I was headed to a Glamor Shots photo shoot than to a fancy restaurant.

I got the final approval from both the cat and Grandma. There was no turning back now. As we made our way back to the kitchen, Catalie Portman peered out my bedroom door and stared at me. "What do you think?" I whispered to her. She seemed to roll her eyes before walking back into my room and jumping up on my bed. I was pretty sure she thought it was a bit much too.

I held my breath as I walked into the kitchen. What would Joe think? As soon as he saw me, his mouth fell open. "Nikki," he finally managed to say. "You look amazing."

Grandma smiled with pride. "You two kids have fun," she said, ushering us out the door with a wink. "But not too much fun."

As soon as we walked in, I was hit with the smell of freshly baked bread and garlic. If I could handcraft my own perfume, this would be it. As we were ushered to the back, I couldn't help but stare at all the pretty tables decorated with fresh roses and candles. Of course, it wasn't really centerpieces I was trying to get a good look at; I wanted to see what people had ordered. But I tried not to let that be too obvious.

Our waiter, Jared, looked like he was twelve. He

pointed out the specials and handed us a wine list. When he walked away and I had a chance to look at the menu, I just stared at it like an idiot. The only thing I'd ever ordered from an Italian restaurant before was spaghetti and pizza. This place didn't appear to have either one.

I looked through the fancy sounding Italian meals and even after reading the descriptions, I still wasn't sure exactly what was in them.

"Oh man," Joe said, reading his menu. "Everything sounds amazing. What looks good to you?"

I scanned the menu again. "I'm thinking about the Fiocchese Con Amaretto." I silently read the description. Beggars' purse ravioli, poached pear, Taleggio cheese, Amaretto pignoli nuts, cream, and garden basil. I didn't know what half of those words meant.

Joe laughed and corrected my pronunciation of the dish. "That sounds great! But it's an appetizer. What are you going to have for your meal?"

I looked at it again and saw that it was under the label "Antipasto." I had thought that meant the foods listed under it were for people who didn't like spaghetti. I thought maybe if I flipped the menu over, I'd find a section called "Antipizzo" for the non-pizza people. Nope. Just desserts.

"I'm not sure," I finally said. "What about you?"

He rattled off some words that sounded extremely sexy and I loved the way his lips moved when he said them. "I'll have that too," I said, putting my menu down.

Joe looked surprised. "You like mussels?"

I picked my menu back up.

When our waiter came back to the table, he seemed like he was in a hurry, which I assumed was because we were nearing his bedtime. Joe ordered his incredible sounding, yet very disgusting, meal and I just pointed to a chicken dish and smiled. "I'll have this." Jared read off the name and even though I was sure he pronounced it right, it didn't sound near as good as if Joe had said it. I nodded and he did a slight eye-roll and walked away.

"This place is beautiful," I said to Joe as I looked around. "Do you come here a lot?"

"Oh no," he said, laughing. "Only when I'm on a date with someone special." He smiled at me and my stomach did a little flip-flop.

I was curious. "So, when was the last time you came here then?"

He could see right through me. "About a year ago. But that's been over for a long time."

I wanted to ask more, but he seemed uncomfortable.

Jared brought us some bread and little dishes with warm garlic-infused olive oil along with our wine. It was delightful.

"So, who was that guy you were with earlier?" Joe peered at me over his piece of bread.

"Les, he's just a friend."

"Does *he* know you're just friends?"

"Yes," I laughed. "Why's that?"

Joe shrugged. "I just saw the way he looked at you. It looked like more than friends to me."

"Well," I assured him. "We *are* just friends. We meet for coffee every once in a while."

We were silent for a minute and then Jared and a redhead with skin as white as our tablecloth brought our meal. One bite of mine and I was thankful I had chosen it. "Would you like a bite?" I asked Joe, cutting a piece of chicken and scooping it and some noodles into the sauce.

I held it out and Joe took a bite. His eyes rolled in the back of his head. "That's amazing. Would you like a bite of mine?"

I looked at his plate full of mussels. "Um, no," I laughed. "I prefer to eat food that's not still in its carcass."

There was still a lingering awkwardness from our conversation about Les and I wasn't sure why. Thankfully, Joe changed the subject.

"So," he said sheepishly. "What's the worst date you've ever been on?"

I laughed. "Honestly, I didn't really date much back home."

He looked surprised. "Really? I figured you've been on lots of dates with six hus..." He stopped mid-word and looked up at me. I was sure his face mirrored my own—sheer terror.

So he knew. Everybody must have known. And I was guessing that meant he knew about Bo too.

I put my fork down, wondering if I should bolt, and if I did, how bad would it be if I ran out with my plate.

"I'm sorry," he said, quickly leaning over the table and trying to grab my hand. I pulled it away and put my hands on my lap. I couldn't even look at him.

"I don't know why I said that."

"Who told you?"

He stammered. "I don't even remember. It really didn't seem like a big deal. I didn't know it was a secret."

I narrowed my eyes at him. "Then why did you stop mid-sentence? Why did you stop if you didn't think it was a big deal?"

He shifted uncomfortably in his chair.

Suddenly something dawned on me. "Oh. My. Gosh. That's why you asked me on this date, isn't it? You saw me with Les and were worried that if you didn't act fast, I'd marry him and you wouldn't get your chance with me."

He looked like a deer caught in headlights.

I shook my head and started to get up. He gently grabbed my arm. "Please," he begged. "That's not it. Don't leave."

I sat back down, not wanting to make a scene.

"Then what is it?"

He stammered. "It's...it's... Okay, if I'm being honest, that's what it was! Okay! I'm not going to lie. I heard you act fast and I wanted to throw my name in the hat. Is that so bad? I like you, Nikki. I didn't want to lose out on a chance to get to know you better."

I didn't know what to say. How could I blame him? Maybe I should have even been flattered in some weird way. But I wasn't. I was embarrassed and angry. And not so much with Joe, but with myself.

"I don't marry people that fast anymore," I finally said. "It's something about me that I'm trying to change... I *am* changing." I couldn't even look at him.

"I don't care about your past," he said, reaching across the table toward me. "I just care about now. Tonight. You and your beautiful hair, and this amazing food, and our waiter that looks like he belongs on a Disney show."

As much as I tried not to, I laughed.

"I've made mistakes too. I have things in my past that I'm not proud of." He sighed and pulled back his hand since I didn't take it. "I was engaged to a girl for four years. Four years! She left me last year and do you know where she is now?"

I shook my head no.

"Ohio. She's married and has a baby on the way. And the part that hurts the most? She married a fireman. And he's Italian! She practically married me. Only it isn't me. And do you know why it isn't me?

145

Because I kept putting off our wedding. I was afraid to actually commit and now she's gone."

My anger and embarrassment faded away as I sat there looking at Joe while he tried to keep himself from falling apart.

He looked up at me with glossy eyes. "I lost her, Nikki. And I know it sounds stupid, but I didn't want to lose my chance with you too."

"So, you would marry me?" I laughed, breaking the sadness that had come over our table.

He smiled. "Are you proposing to me?".

"No! I don't want anything like that for a long time. I just want to take things slow, you know?"

He nodded with a smile. "I don't want to get married that fast either."

I smiled at him and winked. "But four years is a freaking long time, so don't expect to do that again."

That made Joe laugh and just like that, we were back to enjoying our date.

When dessert arrived, I felt like I could finally answer his question that started the whole marriage talk.

"Okay," I said over my tiramisu. "I'll tell you the worst date I've ever been on as long as you promise to tell me yours."

Joe agreed. "I knew you had to have a good one!"

"You can't hold it against me!" I told him. "A couple summers ago, I went on a date to the fair with this guy, Rodney. He wanted to go to the tractor pull..."

"Oh my gosh!" Joe laughed. "That is the worst date ever."

"I haven't even told you the bad part yet!"

"Sorry." He smiled. "Go on."

"So we got our tickets and we're sitting there with our lemonades and all of a sudden, he starts freaking out and pushing me, whispering loudly, 'We have to go! We have to go!' I was like, what is going on? Just tell me already! He pointed to a woman in the row in front of us and down about ten feet. He told me she was his wife and she had a restraining order against him."

"You've got to be kidding me!" Joe said, before laughing. "That's terrible! Please tell me that's not one of the guys you married."

"No," I said, digging in to my dessert, happy to have those days behind me. "They ended up working things out. But I did marry his cousin." I looked up to see if there was any judgement in his eyes, but Joe just laughed harder.

"Okay," I said, leaning over the table a little. "I told you mine, now you tell me yours."

He sighed. "After Julia left me and moved to Ohio, one of my buddies set me up with a friend of his. I picked her up and she was in a bad mood from the get-go. I took her to a Mexican restaurant."

I cringed at that last part.

"I know," he said. "Bad choice for a first date. Never take someone to a restaurant whose bathroom smells like the kitchen. Anyway, no matter what I tried to talk to her about, she just snipped at me. About halfway through dinner, she tells me she's going to the bathroom. So I sit there and sit there and finally I'm really starting to worry about her because she's been gone for nearly twenty minutes, so I text her. She replies back, 'Oh, when I said I had to go to the bathroom, you assumed I meant the one at the restaurant?' Turns out she went home."

"That's just mean!" I laughed.

"Yeah, needless to say that was our last date."

We finished dinner and I was both thankful and surprised that he never mentioned anything about Bo. Maybe he didn't know about him after all. When we got to Grandma Dean's apartment, he opened the car door for me and started to walk me up the sidewalk to her door.

"I didn't know if I should mention this earlier," he said.

Uh oh. That was never good.

"But I stopped for gas before I came by to get you tonight and I ran into Detective Owen at the gas station."

Oh please, tell me he didn't say anything to you about Larry Kramer, I thought.

"Oh?" I asked. "What did *he* have to say?"

He chuckled. "That he wished a group of well-intentioned ladies would stay out of his investigations."

Irene was right, he *was* like a broken record.

"I asked him how the investigation is going and he said something I thought you might find interesting."

Now he had my full attention.

"He said that he was baffled because all the crimes associated with the case happened either between three and three-thirty in the afternoon or late in the evening."

"That *is* weird."

Before I had time to think about it any further, we reached the door. I turned to him and smiled. "Thank you for an...interesting evening."

He took a step closer to me. "Interesting, huh? That's it?"

I shrugged teasingly. "That's it."

He moved a little closer, his body now touching mine. Thanks to my heels, we were eye to eye. "You really do look amazing tonight." He moved a piece of hair out of my face and let his hand linger on my cheek. Then he slid his hand under my hair and held the back of my head, tipping my face toward his.

We had to be less than an inch apart as we looked into each other's eyes. Finally, he moved forward and gently pressed his lips against mine. They were warm and soft. I could hear his breathing quicken as he pressed against me further and deepened his kiss. He had kissed me once before, and even though I had thought that was amazing, it paled in comparison to this.

Suddenly, we were blinded by a bright light that

caught us by surprise. The porch light violently flashed off and on. Grandma Dean.

We both let out a laugh as he pulled away. He touched my face one more time. "I guess that means I should say good-bye."

My heart was still racing and I didn't want our evening to end so soon. "I guess so," I finally said.

He kissed me on the forehead. "I really did have a nice night."

I smiled. "Me too."

I watched him walk down the sidewalk and get into his car. With a deep sigh, I turned and opened the door, expecting Grandma Dean to be standing there, waiting to give me a lecture. But the kitchen was dark. Apparently, she was saving her lecture for tomorrow.

CHAPTER 16

WE LEFT AT NINE THE NEXT MORNING. THE AIR WAS already thick with humidity and it made me feel even more weighed down and exhausted than usual. I had been awake most of the night thinking about Joe. I felt conflicted. For once, I wanted to take things slow and I felt like maybe he didn't. I got the feeling that he was ready to settle down, ready to commit to someone. And for the first time in my adult life, I was on the other end of that spectrum.

"How was your date last night?" Grandma Dean must have been reading my mind as I sat in the passenger seat, silently rehashing my date.

I tried to hide my concerns. "It was fine. The food was amazing! That bread! With that olive oil!" My stomach started to rumble just thinking about it.

Grandma eyed me suspiciously, but thankfully, she didn't ask anything more.

"So, I had an interesting conversation with my friend Delores last night," she said, changing the subject.

"Oh yeah? What was so interesting about it?"

"Remember that man we came across on the sidewalk last week? The one with the heatstroke?"

I nodded.

"Well, it turns out it wasn't heatstroke. He had traces of poison in his system."

I sat up straight. "The killer tried to strike again?" I asked.

Grandma shrugged. "It looks like it, but we can't say for sure."

"Who is the guy? Do you know him? Does he have any connection to Stan or Artie?"

"Delores couldn't tell me his name. She works at the hospital and that could get her fired. But after I got off the phone with her, I did a little snooping and I found out his name is Griffin Meyers. He's a teacher in town. I called Stan and he doesn't know him."

Suddenly, she took a right at a stop sign when she should've taken a left. "You're going the wrong way. We're heading to your antique shop, remember?"

Grandma didn't make eye contact as she answered. "We're making a quick stop first."

Uh oh. I had a feeling I knew where we were headed. Sure enough, we pulled into a neighborhood with towering houses and in front of Larry Kramer's modern-style home.

"Can I just stay in the car?"

She laughed. "Not a chance."

As we made our way up to his front door, I took a deep breath. The night I had run out of Larry's backyard, I had promised myself I would never come back. And yet here I was, standing behind Grandma Dean as she rang the doorbell.

I expected to hear the traditional "ding dong" of the doorbell chiming from somewhere in the house. Instead, I heard what sounded like an auditorium full of people clapping. Grandma and I stood there looking at each other, slightly confused. "That's his doorbell?" I asked.

The door flung open and there stood Larry Kramer, dressed in a suit with a button-down shirt that had the top three buttons undone. His dark chest hair curled around the edges of his shirt, tangling itself in the thick, gold chain that hung below his collar bone. "You like it?" he asked with a sly smile.

Grandma Dean and I looked at each other again, not sure what to say.

"The doorbell sound, I mean."

"Oh yes," Grandma said, clearly relieved. "It's very...ostentatious."

I cringed. That wasn't a compliment.

But Larry beamed and puffed out his chest. "It is, isn't it!"

He looked me up and down, and a cold chill ran up my spine. Even with Grandma Dean standing between us, I still didn't feel safe around this guy. He winked at me. "And to what do I owe the pleasure of your visit?"

I saw Grandma Dean stand up a little taller. She was putting on her game face, summoning all her strength to get this over as quickly as possible. "May we come in?"

Larry smiled and stepped aside, motioning for us to enter. "Of course! I would never turn away two beautiful women. Let's chat in my office."

We walked through the large entryway and I could nearly see the entire layout of his open concept house. A wide backless spiral staircase that looked like it was suspended from the ceiling with cables twirled up to a second floor. The few pieces of furniture had sharp lines and looked like they were made of glass. I didn't see a single piece of furniture that looked like it would be comfortable.

The entryway had a door to the left and one to the right. He led us into the one on the right—his office. His desk was on the opposite side of the room and he crossed over and sat down. He motioned for us to sit on the leather chairs that faced it. As I sat down, I couldn't help but notice the large framed painting of a naked woman, sitting at a table eating an apple.

Larry followed my eyes and turned to look at the painting. "Isn't it beautiful? It's my mother, God rest her soul."

I tried to hide my look of horror, but I'd never been good at that sort of thing. I looked at Grandma and for a split-second, I saw the same look on her face. Thankfully, she recovered before Larry looked at her. "So how can I help you ladies?" he asked.

Grandma cleared her throat. "It was brought to our attention that you know about our little...escapade the other night."

Larry's face took on an overly concerned look. I could tell it was purely for show. He looked at us like we were children and he was the parent. "Yes, I'm sure you had your reasons, but that still gives you no right to pilfer through my things. If you wanted to know something, you should've just come to me. I'd be happy to answer any questions or concerns you have."

Grandma Dean nodded. "I agree, we should've just come to you. And we're all very sorry for our behavior and I can assure you, we won't be so careless in the future."

I thought that was an interesting choice of words. Was she telling him she wouldn't break in again, or she would just be more careful next time so she wouldn't get caught?

"Very well then," he said, his broad smile returning. "All is forgiven, especially since I got something out of it." He winked at me and made a kissy face, then wagged his tongue in the air.

I nearly threw up on his zebra-print rug beneath my feet.

"Since we have you," Grandma said, ignoring his

SHANNON VANBERGEN

crude gesture. "We do have one little question for you...since you said we could ask you anything."

"Shoot," he said, leaning back in his chair and relaxing his hands behind his head.

"When we were here, we noticed a contract on your desk that had Lesus Moore's name on it. And it looked like there was an identical contract behind that with someone else's name on it. Why would two people have a contract for the same location?"

Larry laughed and leaned toward us. "I'll tell you if you promise not to tell."

The wild look in his eyes made my stomach feel sick and I immediately wanted to put my hands over my ears to shield them from whatever Larry was about to say. Unfortunately, I didn't.

"Before I meet with a lady friend, I imagine myself signing a multi-million-dollar deal. It's sort of an aphrodisiac." He laughed a deep, throaty laugh. "I don't need a little blue pill when I can just fill out a contract. It gets me going every time."

"Well," Grandma said, standing up. "I think we've wasted enough of your time today and you've assaulted enough of our senses."

Fear gripped me for a moment. We were seconds from leaving and putting this whole thing behind us and Grandma Dean just had to say something that could upset Larry. I glanced up to see his expression and was surprised, and relieved, to see him smiling. Did anything offend this man?

He stepped around the desk and grabbed my hand as I followed Grandma Dean out of the room. He brought it to his mouth and kissed it slowly. "You come back and see me whenever you want. I'll have an empty contract on my desk, waiting for you. It kicks in before the ink even dries."

I pulled my hand away and ran out of the room nearly as fast as I had run out of his backyard. When we got back to Grandma Dean's car, I opened the glove compartment and pulled out the package of antibacterial wipes.

"I might have to actually cut off this hand!" I said, rubbing it repeatedly with a handful of wipes. "He is the most disgusting man I've ever met in my life."

Grandma reached over. "Hand me a couple. I feel like I need to wipe myself down."

We scrubbed ourselves until we felt like we were sterile, using the entire package of wipes and a few Grandma Dean kept in her purse.

Grandma shuddered. "I was going to stop and get us a coffee, but I think I need something stronger after that visit."

We weren't sure where to get alcohol so early in the morning so we settled on coffee after all. We made a quick stop at the drive-thru at the *Palm Breeze* since we had to pass it on the way downtown to Grandma's antique shop. I sipped on my vanilla frappe and tried to get the images of Larry's naked mother out of my mind.

When we pulled up in front of her store, I tried to remember the last time I had been inside. Probably nearly a month. I had worked there for a little while until Grandma hired someone to take my place so I could devote all my time to opening our newest shop—which sat ready to go, just waiting for us to have time to hold its grand opening.

Grandma unclicked her seatbelt. "Have you met Annalise?"

I shook my head.

"She's a sweetheart. You'll love her."

When we walked in the store, we were greeted by a girl in her late twenties. Her glasses and red hair pulled into a messy ponytail made her look like she belonged more in a bookstore than an antique store.

She smiled at us warmly and her freckles seemed to dance across her cheeks. I liked her instantly.

"Annalise, this is my daughter's daughter, Nikki Rae Parker." Grandma Dean turned to me. "And Nikki, this is Annalise Montgomery. Her father is an accountant and her mother is a schoolteacher."

Grandma Dean always had to give me the low-down on everyone's occupations. It was almost like she thought she was revealing a character trait, something that would help me understand the person better.

"Hi, Nikki," Annalise said cheerfully. "It's nice to finally meet you! I've heard lots of good things about you!"

I stood there awkwardly for a moment. This was usually the part where I would say the same thing back to her…except Grandma Dean never spoke of Annalise and it was just moments ago that I even learned her name.

Grandma spoke up. "We're here to get those items I called you about."

Annalise came out from behind the counter. "Oh yes, I put them over here."

We walked to the back of the store and looked at the collection of furniture Annalise had compiled. I looked at her skinny, white arms and then to the wooden pieces that must of have weighed considerably more than she did. That girl had some muscle tucked in there somewhere.

Grandma pulled out her phone. "I'll call Cliff. He can help us take this to Sydnie's new house."

Annalise didn't question who Sydnie was so I imagined that Grandma Dean had told her all about Stan and his new family. "Excuse me," Annalise said to me when the door jingled, letting us know a customer had arrived. "If you need anything, I'll be up front." She turned and walked away, and I couldn't help but notice that she was dressed more for Illinois weather than for Florida. Her long flowing sweater covered half of her army green leggings, which she had paired with brown leather boots that nearly reached her knees. She must have been one of those types that got cold easily. I couldn't imagine ever being cold in Florida. I hadn't spent a winter here yet though, so maybe I'd be surprised.

I listened to Grandma Dean as she sweet-talked Cliff Sinner, owner of Sinner's Storage, into delivering the furniture to Sydnie's new house.

"He'll be here in twenty minutes," she said when she got off the phone with him. "Let's look around and see if there's anything else Sydnie might need."

We roamed the store, picking up odds and ends here and there—a few bowls, a cute little chair for Lily, a white-washed bookshelf. It wasn't long before Cliff pulled up with a young man and they started to move the furniture to his truck.

"Who's the guy with Cliff?" I asked as we got in Grandma Dean's car to head to Sydnie's house half an hour later.

"That's his son, Greg. Super nice kid, quiet though."

"He seems kind of...weird."

Grandma looked at me in surprise. "Weird? You think something is wrong with everybody!"

"I do not," I protested.

"You thought Les was a killer and thanks to your persistence in the matter, we had to have a very unpleasant talk with Larry this morning."

"No, we had a very unpleasant talk with Larry this morning because Hattie is an idiot."

Grandma shrugged. I had her there.

It took about ten minutes to drive to Sydnie's new

house. I had never been in that neighborhood before and I couldn't help but think that it was a major improvement from her last house, which got me thinking. "What's going to happen to all of Sydnie's things back in Alabama?"

Grandma pulled into the driveway behind Cliff. "Stan said once it's safe for him to leave Hattie's house, they'll go up and get it all."

Suddenly, I remembered Joe's conversation with Detective Owen. "Oh! I almost forgot to tell you! Joe ran into Owen yesterday and Owen said this case really has him stumped."

Grandma sighed. "He's not the only one."

"He also said that all of the crimes have either taken place between three and three-thirty or in the evening. What do you think that means?"

"A killer that only strikes, or attempts to strike, at a specific time…"

"And seems to only be after old men," I added.

"And is willing to use different methods to kill them," Grandma pointed out.

I looked out the window as Cliff opened the back of his truck and started to remove the furniture with the help of his son. "The only other thing we know about him is that he drives a white car."

"I hate to say it," Grandma Dean said with a sigh. "But we might not know anything else until he strikes again."

I shuddered at the thought. I didn't want another

person hurt or killed by that maniac...unless it was Larry Kramer.

TWO HOURS later and thanks to the Grannies, all of whom had also brought their donated household items, Sydnie's house was furnished and looked quite charming. I walked outside and saw Cliff Sinner sitting on the porch steps, clearly exhausted. "Those women are going to kill me one day," he laughed.

I sat down next to him. "How many trips did you make this morning?"

He let out of a slow breath as he thought about his answer. "Too many," he finally said. After he finished unloading the furniture from Grandma's shop, the other Grannies had him make several trips across town to various places to pick up a bed, a table, and a couch. "And from what I hear, they're not done with me yet!"

"Well, that's very kind of you to help out like you have."

He smiled softly. "I'd do anything for your grandmother."

The way he said it made my eyebrows pop up in surprise. I laughed and nudged his arm. "You have a little thing for her?"

His cheeks turned red and I immediately felt bad for teasing him. He clearly did have a thing for her.

Before he had a chance to answer, the Grannies came spilling out the front door.

Irene walked past us, putting her hand on Cliff's shoulder for support as she went down the steps. "Let's go have lunch! I'm so hungry I could eat the south end of a northbound elephant!"

Cliff let out a laugh and stood up. "Even though that's a disgusting metaphor, it's the best suggestion I've heard all day!"

As we made our way to the car, I watched Cliff head to his truck. He said something to his son on the way that made them both laugh. His son seemed a little slow and the way Cliff took him under his wing was touching. Suddenly, it hit me. What if Cliff was the next target? Would it be just a matter of time before we got a call that he had been shot or poisoned? What would happen to Greg if something happened to Cliff? The feeling of fear in the pit of my stomach quickly turned to determination. We needed to find out who was behind all of this, and we needed to do it fast.

CHAPTER 17

WE ARRIVED AT *ROSIE'S CAFÉ* MINUTES LATER. IT WAS A cute little mom and pop restaurant that the Grannies promised me made the best roast beef sandwich in the world.

I was surprised when Rosie herself came to our table to take our order. We had put three tables together to accommodate all of us—five Grannies, myself, Sydnie and Lily, and Cliff and Greg. Just as we walked in, Cliff's daughter Candace was heading inside on her lunch break so Cliff invited her to sit with us too.

"Look at this! A table full of Sinners!" Rosie laughed as she handed each of us a menu.

Sydnie's eyes opened wide and she sat there stunned for a moment.

"I'll let y'all look over the menu and I'll be back with

some waters." Rosie disappeared behind a door in the back.

"I can't believe she said that!" Sydnie's eyes were still wide.

Greta was sitting next to her and put down her menu. "Said what, dear? What's wrong?"

"She called us sinners! Like she's any better than us!"

We couldn't help but laugh.

Greta patted her arm. "She's just referring to Cliff and his kids. That's their last name."

Sydnie still didn't seem so sure.

Cliff let out a joyful laugh at the end of the table. "I've been a Sinner all my life. Born and raised, just like these two!" He reached his arms around his grown kids and pulled them in close.

"Speak for yourself," Candace laughed. "I gave that lifestyle up years ago. I'm a Sullivan now."

Hattie let out a little shriek of laugher. "Once you get to know us a little better, you'll find out that we're all sinners. Some of us more than others."

"Well, if you're not a sinner, you're a hypocrite," Irene said seriously. "Everybody loves a sinner, but nobody loves a hypocrite."

Her comment was met with agreeable nods and soon everyone was busy looking through the menu. Rosie returned with waters and took our orders. I sat there in amazement as she went around the table, listening to everyone's lunch choices and not once writing anything down. I was equally impressed several minutes later when she delivered our meals, everything perfect, clear down to Virginia's choice of cheese and Candace's whole wheat bun, hold the mustard.

As much as I tried to enjoy my roast beef sandwich, which really was the best one I had ever tasted, I worried as the time creeped closer and closer to the time the killer usually struck. I got more and more paranoid with each minute that passed. I eyed every person that came in the café and every car that drove by. Soon, even Lily's cute little antics couldn't take my eyes away from the door or windows.

"You okay?" Grandma Dean's words, even though they were hushed, made me jump in my seat.

"Fine," I said quickly, returning my eagle-eyed stare to the door.

"If you're worried about Sydnie, Stan is paying a bodyguard to keep a close eye on her and Lily."

"Why would someone come after them?" I asked, confused.

Grandma Dean shrugged. "I don't know, but it makes Stan feel better."

I took a deep breath and glanced down at the time. 2:00. That meant I still had at least an hour before we entered the killer's time frame. I was being ridiculous. There were lots of older men that could be targeted. Surely Cliff wouldn't be next. Right?

I started to eat my sandwich again, dipping it in

the now cold little bowl of au jus when two men walked in. One looked vaguely familiar, but I couldn't place him. Apparently, Virginia thought the same thing.

"That guy looks familiar," she whispered to the group. "The way he looked at us makes me think we look familiar to him too."

We watched the two men walk up to the counter. The shorter one turned to look at us and when he saw us staring, he quickly turned back around. The man he was with glared at us for a moment before turning back around himself.

"I know who that is!" Hattie exclaimed. "Geraldine, that's the guy you saved last week! The one with the heatstroke!"

Grandma flashed me a quick look. She must not have told the other Grannies yet about the poison.

"You're right, Hattie!" Greta whispered. "That *is* him!"

Griffin looked much different standing up and conscious than he did laying on the ground half-dead. I was impressed with Hattie for being able to figure out who he was. Even though he was balding, he looked much younger today than he did when he was sprawled out on the sidewalk.

"Hey!" Hattie shouted to him as he walked by with his lunch in a paper bag. "You're looking better!"

The man looked up at us, startled by Hattie's loud greeting.

"Oh yes!" Virginia said. "You've gotten your color back!"

"Who's your friend?" Hattie asked with a wink, nodding to the taller, slightly younger man at Griffin's side.

Griffin finally spoke, his voice a little shaky. "This is my brother, Morris."

We all said hello to Morris, who did nothing more than nod. "Come on," he said gruffly to his brother. "Let's get you home so you can eat your lunch."

Hattie wasn't ready to let them walk away just yet. "How are you feeling?" she asked Griffin.

Griffin shrugged. "Don't have all my energy back yet, but I'm getting there."

Morris pushed Griffin along and spoke to us sharply. "If you ladies will excuse us…"

"What's your hurry?" Irene said. "We could have Rosie add a few more chairs and you could join us. We'd love to get to know you a bit better."

"Oh yes," Hattie said, trying to bat her barely-there eye lashes. "You could sit by me."

Neither Griffin nor Morris seemed interested in Hattie or the lunch invitation. "If you must know," Morris said gruffly, "I have a meeting in forty-five minutes and I need to get Griffin home and settled in. I'm running behind as it is."

Grandma Dean looked at her watch then back up at me. I could tell we were thinking the same thing. "If you don't mind me asking," Grandma said, looking up at them, "what kind of meeting are you headed to?"

Morris furrowed his brows. "I don't know how that's any of your business." With that, he ushered Griffin along and they disappeared out the door.

Grandma Dean leaned close to me. "I don't like that man one bit."

I didn't either, and judging by the looks he gave us as he left, the feeling was mutual. Which was surprising, since Grandma Dean practically saved his brother's life.

"Let's see where he's going," Grandma whispered. With that, she stood and said good-bye to everyone at the table. A chorus of "good-byes" rang out. Lily stole everyone's heart when she waved and blew us kisses with her chubby little hands. That kid was freaking adorable.

We walked outside and saw Morris and Griffin getting in a black Cadillac several cars down. We waited until they pulled out, then carefully followed.

They went through a stop light and we had to stop when it turned red. "We're losing them!" I shouted.

"Calm down," Grandma said, reaching for her phone. "Morris said he was taking Griffin home. We just need to find out Griffin's address." She Googled his name and handed me the phone when the light turned green. "418 Bryant Street. Put that address in the GPS."

I typed it in and we followed the directions to the address. Sure enough, as we pulled up on Bryant Street, we could see the black car pulled over up ahead and Griffin, carrying his paper bag.

Grandma pulled into a driveway a block away and we waited until Morris pulled back onto the road before we started following him again. It wasn't long before I recognized the row of large houses. We had just driven down this street this morning.

"Larry Kramer," Grandma said as Morris pulled into his driveway. "Why do all the roads seem to lead here?" It was more of a rhetorical question but I wondered the same thing. We watched Morris head up the long sidewalk with a briefcase in hand.

"Should we sit here and watch him?" I asked. "See if they come out in a few minutes to go on a killing spree?"

"Couldn't hurt," Grandma said, settling back in her seat.

A few minutes of silence and I was already bored out of my mind. "We've never really talked about this but...what do you think about Stan marrying Sydnie? I mean, she was, like, fifty years younger than him."

Grandma shrugged a little. "He's an adult, he can do what he wants. I try not to judge."

"Oh come on! Fifty years older! That's crazy! And he doesn't seem like the kind of guy who would do that! That makes him a..." I stopped. What did that make him? "What do you call a male version of a cougar?"

Grandma thought about it. "A man," she laughed.

"Men can get away with stuff like that. Now if *I* married a man in his early twenties..." She didn't even finish her sentence, just trailed off in laughter. "I think it was a marriage of convenience for both of them," she continued. "Though I do think that Stan loved her. Sydnie... I think she loved his money."

"And don't you think it's crazy how quickly she came to live here?" I pressed. "She literally walked out of her door, with complete strangers, minutes after meeting us! Who does that?"

Grandma took a deep breath and I could tell she was trying to pick her words carefully, though I couldn't understand why at first. "So, what you're telling me," she finally said, "is that you're questioning why a woman would make such poor choices in who they marry, and then run away from their life, leaving everything behind? Doesn't that remind you of someone?"

Ouch.

"But I knew you! I didn't leave with strangers!" I objected once I recovered from the sting.

Grandma stared out the front window. "She obviously wanted to get out of her current situation. It's hard to raise a child on your own, on one income, especially when you look out your window and see the rest of the world going by and you're stuck inside with a heart full of broken dreams, unpaid bills, and a pile of dirty diapers."

Her words struck me. Was she still talking about

Sydnie, or herself? Was that why she left my mother to go to Europe? She felt trapped?

Grandma Dean snapped out of her little daydream and turned to me with a weak smile. "I try not to judge. You never really know what people are going through."

We sat there quietly for another twenty minutes before I couldn't take it anymore. "Umm, I hate to end this fun, but I have to use the bathroom."

"Seriously?" Grandma asked.

I nodded.

Grandma sighed and put the car in drive. "You're the worst stakeout partner ever. We didn't even make it half an hour."

"Well, if I would've known we were going to do this, I wouldn't have finished off my second lemonade at lunch."

"Always be prepared for a stakeout," Grandma said, pulling on to the road. She glanced at me. "You're learning a lot of valuable things today. You should be writing them down."

I picked up my phone and pretended to type as I spoke out loud. "What I learned today... Try to anticipate and prepare for Grandma's every move."

Grandma Dean laughed. "That's about right. And stop calling me Grandma. It makes me sound old."

CHAPTER 18

"GOOD MORNING," GRETA SAID AS SHE ENTERED Grandma's kitchen the next day. She held up a container. "I made some sugar cookies for Lily and I was going to run them by. Do you ladies want to come along?"

Grandma Dean and I had plans to head to our new shop and prepare for the grand opening we had pushed back yet another week. I had some marketing ideas I was excited to share with her. Grandma looked at Greta, then at me, and I knew our plans would have to wait.

Soon we were out the door and headed toward Grandma Dean's car. "Isn't it a little too early for cookies?" Grandma asked.

Greta was indignant. "It's never too early for cookies, is it, Nikki?"

"Nope. As a matter of fact, if you'd like me to do a quick quality check, I'd be happy to do that for you."

Greta stopped and opened the lid. Puffy cookies in the shape of hearts, covered in pastel pink frosting, filled the container. I took one and sunk my teeth into it. It practically melted in my mouth. I suddenly wished I had the cookie-making kind of Grandma instead of the always-wear-lip-gloss-and-mascara-and-always-be-classy type.

"Good?" Greta asked.

"Delicious," I said through a mouthful of sugary goodness.

She smiled with pride.

"Nikki doesn't need any more sugar," Grandma Dean scolded her. "She eats enough for us all."

Greta looked at me and rolled her eyes. Then she pulled out one more cookie and handed it to me with a wink as Grandma walked ahead of us.

"Don't think I didn't see that," Grandma said without turning around.

As we pulled onto Sydnie's street, Greta was turned around in the front seat, showing me the latest pictures she had taken of Lily. "And here she is after you guys left lunch yesterday. She was eating her ice cream. And this is her sitting in that little chair you guys brought over for her. Oh, and I love this one…"

Grandma Dean suddenly gasped. Greta turned around to look out the front window and I tried to lean between the two front seats to see what had Grandma speechless. Greta and I must have seen it at the same time, because we both let out a gasp that echoed Grandma's.

Standing at the bottom of the steps that led up to Sydnie's house was Sydnie, and she wasn't alone. Her arms were wrapped around a very large man—not large in the weighty sense, but large as in he could bench-press a rhinoceros.

"Who's that?" Greta asked with her hand over her mouth.

"I think that's Sydnie's new bodyguard," Grandma Dean said with disgust.

I watched her practically clinging to the man, though I couldn't blame her. Even from this far back, you could tell he was a very good-looking man. And he was obviously much closer to her age than Stan. "Well, it looks like he's definitely doing *something* with her body, though I'm not sure I'd call it guarding."

We drove by slowly, not even attempting to hide the fact that we were gawking.

Greta sat back in her seat. "Well, that didn't take her long," she spat. "We need to tell Stan."

"What exactly do we tell him?" Grandma asked. "That we saw them hugging? That doesn't really seem like something bad."

Just then, we saw Sydnie stand on her tiptoes and kiss the guy.

"No, but that does!" Greta said.

Poor Stan. I didn't think he was going to take the news well.

We drove down Sydnie's street in silence, except for Greta who would occasionally make a "tsk tsk" sound. I could tell she was silently shaming Sydnie for two-timing Stan.

"So, what do you think?" Grandma asked us. "Do you think Sydnie is behind all of this? Do you think she somehow put out a hit on Stan?"

"I don't want to believe it," Greta said. "But it makes sense, doesn't it?"

"Honestly," Grandma said, turning toward the retirement village, "I'm so emotionally wrapped up in this, I can't think straight. And that's not like me, not like any of us."

"It's because of Lily," Greta said sadly. "We've never worked a case that involved a child before. That sweet little thing has us all distracted."

A few minutes later, we were back at the retirement community. Grandma sighed. "Should we all go in and tell him?"

Greta agreed. She looked down at the container of cookies on her lap. "I suppose I can give him these— maybe they will soften the blow a little."

As much as I loved her cookies, I didn't think they would be enough to mend a broken heart.

We walked up to Hattie's door and said hello to the police officer still stationed outside. Greta handed him a cookie and he took it with a smile. "Grandma Greta's famous sugar cookies," he said with a smile. "My favorite!"

Greta beamed. I imagined she kept the guy well-fed.

Hattie opened the door and blinked into the sun. "It's so bright out here! Come in, come in." We walked into her kitchen, which felt like it was the same temperature as outside. I didn't know how that woman could stand it being so hot.

Hattie leaned close to Grandma Dean. "Look at my eyes! Are they still green or are they turning white?"

Grandma backed away, trying to reclaim her personal space. "They're green, Hattie. Why would they be white?"

"Because I feel like I'm turning into one of those little creatures that live in caves. You know the ones, they're all white and completely blind because you don't need your eyesight in the dark."

"Like a salamander?" Greta asked. "I saw that on the Discovery Channel one time."

"Yes!" Hattie exclaimed. "Like a blind little salamander! Or a cave cricket! That's what that man has reduced me to!"

"Well, turn on a light," Grandma exclaimed as she walked into the living room and flipped on the overhead light.

Stan came flying out of his bedroom. "I heard a light-switch! Who turned on a light!"

We gasped when we saw him. Stan looked frail, and we had never seen him so paranoid.

Grandma softened her tone and reached out to him. "Stan, it's okay. There's an officer right outside. You're safe in here."

He looked around frantically and didn't seem to believe her. If he was already like this, he wasn't going to take the latest news well.

"Stan, we need to talk to you about something." Grandma took him by his good arm, the other one still in a bandage, leading him to a chair and motioning for him to sit.

Hattie looked at us, concerned. "Do you have news about the case?"

"We might. At first, we felt like somehow Larry Kramer was involved, though we couldn't figure out how. But the more Nikki and I talked about it, we think he might actually be innocent. Yes, he's a complete dirt bag, but he does a lot of business in town so maybe that's why his name keeps popping up."

Hattie looked confused. "So, who do you think is behind this then?"

Grandma looked at Greta and I, and when neither of us spoke up, she took a deep breath. "Stan, I hate to be the one to tell you this, but we think it's Sydnie."

Stan leaned forward and what little color he had drained from his face. "What? Why would you think that?"

"We just drove by to check on her and we saw her." Greta stopped, not wanting to go on, but to my surprise, she did. "And she was embracing her bodyguard."

"It does makes sense," Hattie said. "She was after your money before and maybe she wants it again."

"But you can hardly blame her, Stan," Greta said quickly. "You should've seen the place her and Lily were living in before. That's not a place for a little one. I think all this is just her ill attempt to get money from you to take care of Lily."

"So, she hired someone to kill me? To get my money?" Tears filled Stan's eyes. "How would she even be able to do that?"

"It's the internet," Hattie said. "It will be the death of us all. Just you wait and see!"

Stan rested his head in his hands and we all sat there silently. Finally, he lifted his head. "So, what do I do now?"

"I think we call your attorney," Grandma Dean said firmly. "We invite Sydnie to a meeting with him and you offer her money to go back to Alabama and take care of Lily."

"You want me to just pay her off and let her take Lily out of my life for good?" Stan could barely get the words out.

"It's either that or you continue living like this." Grandma waved her arm around the living room.

Stan looked at the carpet and closed his eyes as he thought it over. "I'll call Harry right now. I'll have to move some money around, but I can give her enough that her and Lily can live comfortably for a while."

It broke my heart to see Stan like this. He left the room and even though I couldn't tell exactly what he was saying, I could hear his muffled voice as he talked to his attorney.

When he emerged a few minutes later, his eyes were red. "It's done. We'll meet at three."

I didn't like the time and obviously, neither did Grandma Dean. "Couldn't he meet with you earlier... or later?"

Stan didn't answer. He just plopped himself down in a chair in the living room.

Greta headed to the front door. "I'll let the officer know you're leaving this afternoon and to follow us to your lawyer's office."

"No, don't!" Stan flew out of the chair. "Don't tell him."

Greta looked at all of us and we were all surprised by Stan's reaction.

"Why not?" Greta asked. "It's his job to protect you."

Stan shook his head. "If I walk out that front door, I'm a sitting duck. I can't bring any attention to the fact that I'm leaving. You guys need to sneak me out the back door. If the killer is out there, he'll be watching the front door, waiting for the officer to escort me somewhere. We can't let anyone know I'm leaving. By the time we leave the meeting, hopefully Sydnie will have called this whole thing off."

Grandma shook her head. "Stan, I don't like this plan."

"Well," he said, his voice firm. "I don't like this *situation,* but I guess we're all just going to have to deal with it."

Not only did Stan not like *that* situation, but he didn't like the one that came a few hours later either.

CHAPTER 19

"I'M NOT WEARING THAT," HE SAID TO GRANDMA DEAN.

"It's the only thing we have that fits you. Now put it on."

He trudged into the bathroom and came out a few minutes later. Grandma and Greta tried not to snicker, but Hattie let loose. "I need to take a picture of this for Virginia! Won't she be surprised at how well you fit into her dress."

"No pictures," Grandma said, holding up her hand. "This is hard enough without you making fun of the poor guy."

"Well, it's his own fault," Hattie said defensively. "We could all just walk out the front door, but NO! He has to go incognito out the back."

"It's the safest way," Stan said quietly.

None of us were sure it was.

Greta handed him another piece to his costume. "Here, put this on."

Stan sighed and took the wig. He put it on his head, but he didn't seem to have it on right. Grandma Dean fixed it then stepped back and looked at him. "Do you want any makeup?"

"Certainly not," he said gruffly. "This is humiliating enough."

"Well," Hattie said, handing him a pair of Virginia's flats. "This is the last piece of your outfit. You should be thankful Virginia is such a Yeti and you can wear her clothes."

"That's not very nice," Greta said. "Maybe Virginia is the perfect size and we're all just short!"

"Nope," Hattie said. "That woman can practically change the light bulbs on her ceiling fan sitting on her couch!"

"She's not that tall," Grandma Dean said, adjusting Stan's wig again. "But I am thankful she could run something by for Stan." Grandma sighed. "Okay, you ready to do this?"

Stan nodded and put on Virginia's shoes.

"You two riding along?" Grandma asked Hattie and Greta. They looked at each other and it was clear they weren't.

Greta reached out and held on to Stan's arm. "I think it's best if this is just a family affair. I'll be right here for you when you get back."

Hattie looked at Stan and huffed. "I just don't want to get shot."

We all flashed Hattie our usual disappointed look, but I figured we all felt the same way—we just weren't rude enough to say it.

We snuck Stan out the back door and walked along the pool area until we reached the back gate. Grandma Dean had moved her car earlier and got as close to that area as she could. I got in the front seat and Stan sat in the back. The drive to the lawyer's office was mostly silent until Grandma asked about Sydnie. "Did you tell her why you wanted her to meet you at your lawyer's office?"

Stan looked out the window and watched the world go by as we drove down Main Street. He sighed. "I made it sound like it was about buying a house. She sounded excited. Her bodyguard will be bringing her."

Sadness tugged at my heart. The last week had been a roller coaster for all of us, but I couldn't imagine what it was like for Stan.

We got there before Sydnie did and Stan made a beeline for the bathroom to change out of Virginia's clothes. When he came back out, Stan's lawyer, Harry Berkshire led us to a large room. He gave us all expensive-looking bottled waters, but none of us opened them. Instead, we left them sitting in front of us on the large wooden table. Every time one of us shifted in our seats, the leather beneath us would squeak, adding to the awkwardness in the room.

It wasn't long until Sydnie walked in carrying Lily. Her smile vanished when she saw Grandma and I sitting on either side of Stan. "What are they doing here?" she asked, her voice concerned.

Stan couldn't speak. Instead, he sniffed and Grandma reached over to take his hand.

"What's going on?" Sydnie asked, her eyebrows furrowed in concern.

'The gig is up,' I wanted to say. But I had a feeling she knew that.

"Down, down." Lily's tiny voice seemed to echo in the room as she squirmed in her mother's arms. She fought to get down, reaching out for Stan. It was almost too much for the poor man to bear.

"Would you like for me to take Lily outside?" I offered, standing up.

"No, what I would like is for someone to tell me what's going on here."

Harry put his hand on her back and led her into the room and to a chair. "If you'd sit down, we can get started."

I was thankful that Harry was taking the lead. As soon as Sydnie sat down, Harry started. "Stan is offering you a very generous amount of money so you can go back to Alabama and take care of your daughter."

Stan let out a sound that sounded like a muffled whimper. Lily looked at him and reached out her arms to him. Stan buried his face.

"And why would he do that?" Sydnie asked angrily.

"Because it has been brought to our attention that you have ulterior motives for being here," Harry continued. "And we feel it's in Stan's best interest if you take this very kind offer and leave immediately." He slid a sheet of paper to Sydnie and she looked at the amount typed onto it. I couldn't see exactly what it was from my chair across the table, but I could tell there were several numbers involved.

"If you sign the contract stating that you'll call off any…ill plans you may have toward Stan, we can wire you the money by this afternoon." Harry held out his pen and waved it a little when Sydnie didn't take it right away.

"Is this what you want?" Sydnie asked Stan.

"Yes," he said quietly.

Lily squirmed even more on Sydnie's lap. "Down, down" she said again, reaching for Stan. But her words seemed different. When she repeated it again, we realized she wasn't saying "down," she was saying "Dad."

Stan couldn't take it anymore. He got up and ran out of the room.

"I hope you're happy!" Grandma Dean yelled at Sydnie. "You've broken that man's heart more than once! But I can promise you this, it will be the last time!" Grandma ran out after Stan.

Harry pushed the paper closer to Sydnie. "All you

have to do is sign this and all of your troubles will be over."

Sydnie pushed away from the table and spun Lily around, putting her over her shoulder. "I'm not signing anything. It's true, I don't love him, and I know he doesn't love me. But I thought he could love Lily." Her voice cracked. She backed away from the table, then stood there for a second. I thought she was going to walk out, but instead, she leaned over and signed the paper.

"You'll call off any plans to hurt Stan?" Harry asked matter-of-factly.

She narrowed her eyes at us. "I would never hurt Stan."

"No," I said. "But you would hire someone to kill him."

"You people are crazy," she said. She turned to Harry. "Make sure I have that money this afternoon so I can get out of here as soon as possible."

He nodded and Sydnie stormed out of the room.

I thanked Harry for his time and walked outside to the parking lot. Sydnie had just finished buckling Lily in her car seat and she glared at me one more time before she got in the passenger side of her bodyguard's black SUV.

I looked at Grandma Dean, who was standing outside of her car, her face completely white. I could see Stan sitting in the back sobbing.

Grandma met me at the front of the car. "I talked to

the bodyguard while you and Sydnie were still in Harry's office." Her face was twisted with concern.

"What did he say?"

"I confronted him about the hug. He said that Lily had wandered off and he found her in the neighbor's yard. He said that even though Sydnie had been flirtatious the last two days, the hug was because Sydnie was thankful he had found Lily. That's it. Nothing more."

"And the kiss?"

Grandma sighed. "He claims he doesn't remember it."

I took a deep breath. Did we really just jump to conclusions and ruin things for Stan? I looked up at Grandma Dean. "She signed the papers," I said slowly. "So maybe she's guilty after all."

Grandma shrugged. "I just hope this whole thing is over with."

As we got in the car, it started to rain. Grandma immediately turned the windshield wipers on full blast, expecting the usual torrential downpour that seems to happen every other afternoon here. It would probably be over before we even got home.

As we drove away, I glanced back at Stan. His head was back against the seat and was tilted so he could look out the window. He seemed to be watching the rain as it slid down the glass. The dark sky made the mood that much more somber as Grandma Dean drove silently through town.

I leaned my head against my seat and closed my eyes. I wished the squeak of the windshield wipers would drown out the sound of Lily's voice in my head calling out "Dad."

Suddenly, I heard tires squeal. They sounded so close that I bolted upright, expecting to see a car right outside the window. I didn't see a car, but instead, I heard a sound that was ear-shattering. For a moment, all I could hear was a loud ringing in my ears. I could see Grandma Dean shouting something but I couldn't make out the words. Then all at once, the sound came rushing back and Grandma was screaming, "Take a picture! Take a picture!"

I looked into the backseat and Stan was covered in blood. His window had been shot out and he was yelling something I couldn't understand. I grabbed my phone and took a picture. I was shaking so badly I didn't know if the picture would turn out or if it would just be one big blur.

"Text that to Owen," Grandma yelled. "Tell him we're headed to the hospital. Stan's been shot!"

I tried to send it, but I was shaking so badly that I had to try several times to hit the send button. As the message went through, I noticed the time on my phone. 3:23.

It seemed like it took forever to get to the hospital. I ran in the emergency entrance and explained what happened. Within seconds, Stan was loaded onto a stretcher and rushed inside. Grandma was already on the phone with the Grannies, telling them to get to the hospital as quickly as possible.

Grandma and I stood in the emergency room waiting area and held each other as we cried. "Sydnie must have called the hit man when we left the lawyer's office." I sniffed. "She wanted all of his money, not just whatever he offered her."

Detective Owen came up behind us. He was out of breath and I imagined it was from him running through the hospital. "What's going on?"

Grandma spun around and looked at him. "What are you doing here?" she yelled. "Why aren't you tracking down those license plates?"

"What license plates?" he yelled back.

"The one Nikki sent you in the picture!"

Detective Owen looked at me, confused. He pulled out his phone and turned it around so Grandma could see. "She didn't send me a picture of plates. She sent me this."

Grandma looked from Owen's phone to me, clearly disappointed.

"What?" I yelled, looking at the picture of Stan, bloody and screaming in the backseat. "You told me to take a picture!"

"I meant of the car where the shots came from! It was right there!"

I could barely make out the corner of a white vehicle on the far side of the picture. Had I turned the camera just a little more to the right, I would've gotten, albeit accidentally, the picture Grandma had intended.

She dropped her hands, exasperated.

Owen looked at us sternly. "I'm going to make some phone calls. You two don't go anywhere."

Hattie, Greta, and Virginia came bursting through the doors and ran up to Grandma Dean.

"How is he?" Greta asked.

"We don't know anything yet. But he was conscious when we got here." Grandma's voice cracked.

They hugged and Greta pulled away. "Someone should call Sydnie."

"Why would we call her?" I asked. "She's the one behind this."

"I don't think she is," Greta said. "She called me when she left the lawyer's office. She said she was leaving this afternoon and wanted to know if I wanted to come and say good-bye to Lily."

At least Sydnie was capable of doing *something* nice.

Hattie pulled out her phone. "I recorded the conversation in case we needed to use it against her later." These old ladies were very tech-savvy.

We gathered around Hattie's phone and she hit play. We could see Greta with her phone out in front of her. She had it on speaker and we could clearly hear Sydnie's voice. She was sobbing. "Why would he send me away?" she was asking. "Why doesn't he want to be a part of Lily's life?"

Greta could be seen on the phone wiping away a

tear. "Because, dear, you hired a hitman to kill him. What do you expect him to do?"

"I didn't do that!" Sydnie cried. "Why would I do that?"

We could see Greta take a deep breath. "For his money."

There was more crying from Sydnie. "You guys are the ones that came and got me. I never even tried to get in contact with Stan!"

We all hung over the phone, listening to Sydnie sob.

"That doesn't sound like someone who is guilty," Greta said. "I don't think she had anything to do with it."

"She was a street actress," I protested. "Remember when she told us that?"

"Shhh," Hattie said. "There's more."

We brought our attention back to the phone.

"Geraldine told me you took the money," Greta said softly into the phone. "She sent me a text and told me."

"Of course I did," Sydnie cried. "How else will I get home? I have nothing, Greta! That was fine when I was at least surrounded by my friends in Fairhope. But here, I have nothing, no one! What else was I supposed to do?"

I started to get a sick feeling in the pit of my stomach. I believed her. I believed she was innocent.

"You can keep listening but there's just more crying," Hattie said. "Until someone pulls up at her house and she gets off the phone."

"Someone was there? Who was it?" Grandma questioned. "Sydnie said herself she doesn't know anyone here."

Greta shrugged. "I guess it was the bodyguard."

"The bodyguard was with her at the lawyer's office. Hit play again!" Grandma ordered.

Greta hit play and we froze when Sydnie said, "I have to go. A white car just pulled up in the driveway and some man is walking up."

Grandma Dean and I looked at each other. "Sydnie's in trouble."

A nurse came out and walked up to our group. "Is anyone here family?"

As the other Grannies tried to lie and say they were his sisters, Grandma Dean and I snuck out. I didn't see Owen so I sent him a text telling him we thought Sydnie might be in trouble.

When we walked outside and saw that Grandma's car was surrounded by policemen, my heart fell. "Now what?" I asked. She smiled at me and dangled a set of keys I didn't recognize.

"I took these from Virginia," she said with a sly smile. "Now we just have to figure out where she parked."

We walked up and down several aisles, Grandma hitting the lock button on the phone, hoping to hear Virginia's SUV beep in response. Finally, we heard the sound we were hoping for and saw headlights flash. We found her vehicle.

We climbed in and quickly made our way to Sydnie's house. When we turned on her street, we could see a white car parked in her driveway. Grandma quickly pulled in behind it and I looked at the car confused.

"Why is Les here?" I asked.

"What? Where is he?" Grandma asked, looking around.

"I don't know, but that's his car." I pointed to the car in front of us.

"That's not Les's car, Nikki." Grandma was yelling at me for some reason. "That's the one I saw before Stan got shot!

"It *is* his!" I yelled back. "There's a Peace Pointe Community College bumper sticker on the back. Les has been taking classes there!"

Grandma looked at the bumper sticker, then up to the house. "We need to find out what's going on."

She took off her seatbelt and marched up to the door, I followed close behind her, not nearly as sure of myself as she was. When we made it to the door, Grandma barged in. I looked behind us into the street, hoping I would see police cars making their way toward us, or at the very least, Owen. But no one was there.

"What in the world?" Grandma Dean's words made me swing back around. I looked past her and into the living room. The bodyguard lay on the floor, bleeding from his head. A terrified Sydnie stood on the far side of the living room and Griffin Meyers stood to her left.

"What's going on?" Grandma demanded.

Sydnie was shaking.

"Where's Lily?" Grandma asked.

"I shut her in her room," Sydnie cried. "She's safer in there."

"Shut up!" Griffin yelled, his voice still a little shaky. "I can't handle all of this crying!"

Grandma narrowed her eyes at him. "You're the one after Stan? But why?"

"This is for the greater good," Griffin yelled as he waved the bloody baton in the air. "With the old man gone and no heir to claim his money, it will all go to the community college."

Suddenly, a piece of the puzzle fell into place. I remembered the newspaper article a week or so ago about budget cuts and layoffs at the college. Griffin was going to lose his job. "So, this is all over you losing your job?" I stated more than asked.

"I can't lose my job! I just signed a contract to build a house and if I don't have a job, I won't be able to pay for it!"

"So, Larry Kramer *is* involved in this after all," I declared smugly.

"Yeah, the jerk won't let me out of my contract. He's already cashed my check and won't give me my money back," he moaned. "My brother even tried to persuade him, but he still wouldn't budge. I'm completely broke and they've already cut back on some of the classes I teach."

Another piece of the puzzle came together in my mind. And that piece involved Les's car. It wasn't leaking gas like Les had suspected. It was being driven without his knowledge. That also explained the timing —all the crimes happened when Les was either in his afternoon or evening class.

"I can't believe you would steal Les's car!" I yelled. "A teacher, stealing from a student while they're in class!"

"Well, I certainly wasn't going to try to kill someone driving my own car!"

That was actually pretty smart on his part.

"Enough of this chatter!" Griffin yelled. He held the baton above Sydnie's head and suddenly brought it down hard. It skimmed the side of her face, hitting her on the shoulder instead.

"Ow!" she cried out, clutching her shoulder.

How in the world had this guy managed to kill one man and wound another? Of course, he had killed the wrong man and failed multiple times to kill his intended victim. And then it hit me—the last piece of the puzzle. I nearly laughed out loud.

"The poison," I cried out. "You weren't poisoned. You poisoned *yourself* on accident!"

I probably should have known better than to provoke a homicidal maniac, but I couldn't help myself. I could tell I had hit the mark, though, because he turned red and looked like he wanted to run away and hide.

Grandma decided it was time to kick him while he was down. "You're a pathetic little man."

I cringed, afraid that might push him over the edge, but he just hung his head. "I know. And I didn't mean to kill Stan's friend," he finally said. "I have terrible aim."

"It's a good thing," Grandma said, "otherwise Stan would be dead too."

"Stan's still alive?" Griffin's head jerked up in surprise.

"You shot him in the arm," Grandma said. "He's going to be just fine."

I saw a look in his eyes that scared me, but before I could act, Sydnie lunged forward.

"You shot Stan?" she cried. "You monster!"

She tried to tackle Griffin and he swung the baton wildly, trying to defend himself. Grandma Dean and I ran to Sydnie's side and then all of a sudden I heard— and felt—a crack, and the whole front of my face lit up in pain. For a moment, I thought I even saw little birds flying around my head like in the cartoons. Griffin had missed Sydnie and hit me instead. I grabbed my face and fell over backward onto the bodyguard, who was still lying unconscious and motionless on the living room floor.

Just as I managed to sit up, the back door burst open.

I looked over my hands, which I had clasped over my nose, just as Hattie reached into her purse and pulled out a rope. Within seconds, she had Griffin on the ground, hog-tied. She stood up. "Time?"

Greta hit a button on her phone. "Eleven seconds."

"Darn it, tied my record. I really thought I had it that time."

"How did you guys get here?" Grandma asked.

"My car," Irene said. "Though we would've been here sooner if we'd realized quicker that you stole Virginia's SUV! We walked around the parking lot for five minutes before we realized it was gone and she hadn't just forgotten where she parked it!"

Suddenly, the front door swung open and we all jumped. Detective Owen and several other officers barged through the door, guns drawn. "Everybody freeze!" he shouted.

He took a second to scan the room. I was sitting on the bodyguard, who was unconscious from a head wound, my nose bleeding down my face and onto my shirt. Griffin was on his stomach with his hands and feet tied behind his back while the Grannies and Sydnie stood next to him with their hands up. In the silence, we could hear little Lily's voice calling from her room. "Mama," she cried.

"What is going on in here?" Owen demanded, shaking his head.

Lily's voice called out again.

"Can I go get her?" Sydnie pleaded.

Owen waved her on and she quickly ran out of the room.

I tried to get off the bodyguard, but the room started spinning and I sat back down again. Grandma Dean rushed to me as the officers put their guns away.

Hattie bent down to get a good look at me. "You broke your nose."

"Yeah," I said irritably. "I know."

She patted me on the back. "It's a good thing. You really needed a new one anyway."

───

WHEN I GOT to the hospital, Joe was waiting for me in the emergency room. He took a look at me and grimaced. "Ouch!"

"You're telling me," I said, my hand still over my nose.

"You can let go of your nose," Hattie said to me. "It's not like you're holding back the blood."

"I know," I said through my hand. "But I feel like my hand is the only thing holding my nose on."

Hattie huffed. "You're being awfully dramatic."

"She's not being dramatic," Grandma dean defended me. "She's being theatrical." She looked at me. "And you're doing a very good job of it."

I tried to roll my eyes, but my face hurt too bad. I looked at Joe. "How did you know I was here?"

"Owen called me."

From across the room, I saw Owen. He was questioning Sydnie. He looked at me and smiled gently.

A doctor called my name and Grandma came and took my arm. "I'm going to go back with you," she said, smiling.

My heart swelled with love for her. "Thank you." I said, starting to cry.

"You're welcome," she said softly. "Someone needs to help you pick out a better nose."

EPILOGUE

"Hello, beautiful!" Grandma's voice rang out as another customer walked into our shop.

"I was beginning to think this day was never going to happen," Grandma Dean said to me as she rang up a customer and put two tiny cat tutus into a pink bag. "We're having an even better turnout than I had hoped!"

I looked around at the shop full of customers. Everyone was talking and laughing and enjoying themselves. The designer cat clothes were a big hit. Kitty Purry strutted through the store in her bright blue shirt with a skirt that was made out of peacock feathers. She was enjoying the attention while Catalie Portman hid behind the counter, out of the spotlight.

Suddenly, I heard a voice that made my blood curdle.

"Good morning, ladies." I looked up to see Larry Kramer holding a cat bikini. "Since your little investigation is over, I'm guessing that means I won't be seeing you on a professional level anymore."

"That's right," Grandma Dean said with a smile. "You won't have to worry about us sneaking in your house anymore. And I'm sorry we thought you were involved."

Larry laughed. "I'm honored you would think I could've been involved in something so dastardly. But, just so you know, I'm not nearly as bad as you think I am. I gave Griffin a full refund. Maybe now his brother will stop harassing me about it. The house he's going to is going to be much bigger than the one I was going to build for him anyway."

"To think," Grandma said dryly, "that if you just would've done that from the beginning, none of this would've happened and Artie would still be alive."

Larry shrugged. "But then we'd still have to deal with Artie."

"And Stan never would've met Lily," I pointed out.

"See!" Larry said. "My actions brought a family together. That practically makes me a saint."

Grandma rolled her eyes and rang up the cat bikini. "I didn't know you had a cat," she said to Larry.

"Oh, this is a for a cat?"

Grandma handed him the bag before he could change his mind.

He took it and leaned over the counter. "Don't

forget about me," he whispered to me. "I still have a contract waiting for you. And," he said, lifting his pink bag, "I have a little outfit for you to wear." He winked and turned to walk out the door.

"That's the creepiest person I've ever met," I said to Grandma as she straightened up a display of cat bows that sat on the counter.

"Me too," she said under her breath.

By afternoon, I thought nearly all of Peace Pointe had come into the shop to say hello and congratulate Grandma Dean and I on opening our new store. But then I saw Sydnie and Stan standing outside on the sidewalk and I realized there were still a few residents who hadn't made it in yet.

Stan looked twenty years younger as he opened the door for Sydnie, who was carrying Lily. He strode in confidently and I was amazed at his transformation. It had been two weeks since I had last seen him, bloody and screaming in the backseat of Grandma's car.

"Geraldine, this place looks great," he said as he made his way over to us.

Grandma smiled and gently hugged him. "Thank you. How's your arm?"

"It's better," he said. "You know it takes a little while for us old folks to heal, but it's doing pretty good."

"You're not old," Sydnie said to him, resting her head on his arm and giving him a gentle hug herself, "you're vintage. And vintage is very cool right now."

Stan laughed and Grandma Dean tried not to roll her eyes.

I helped a customer while Grandma chatted with Stan and Sydnie, and I watched Lily squirm out of her mother's arms and walk over to look at some cat toys in a basket on the floor. She picked one out and Stan brought it up to the counter to pay for it.

"We're getting Lily a cat," he said to me as he pulled out his wallet. "She loves animals."

"That's great," I said with a smile. "I'm so glad that everything worked out for you."

"Me too," he said, looking at Lily. "I don't have a lot of time with her, but I can promise you, I'll make the most of every second."

I handed him his bag and we said our good-byes. Then Stan reached down to take a hold of Lily's hand and, as they walked away, Lily held out her free hand to her mom. Sydnie gently took it, looking up at Stan and smiling. They walked toward the door, laughing and lifting Lily in the air.

With the sun coming in through the front windows, all I could see was their silhouettes as they left. It showed no signs of age, just the outline of a mom, a dad, and a very loved little girl.

A shiver went down my spine. To think that one terrible man almost took all that away. And he did it because of money. But was it really money, I thought. Or was it fear that drove Griffin to attempt to murder someone? Fear of losing his job, fear of losing his house. And really, weren't a lot of crimes committed because someone was afraid? Afraid of not having enough money, afraid of someone having more, afraid of someone else striking first... Greed, murder, corruption. The root of all evil might be money, but maybe the seed is fear.

Thanks for reading *The Root of All Evil*. I have a lot of fun writing the Glock Granny's books and I hope you have fun reading them!

If you enjoyed this book, it would be great if you left a review for me on Amazon and/or Goodreads. That will really help me tell others about the book because Amazon shares books that have a lot of reviews with more people.

The next book in the series is called *All in the Family* and it is available now. Grab your copy today!

At the end of the book, I have included some poetry from Lesus Moore as well as a recipe for Greta's Famous Sugar Cookies (they're delicious).

I have also included previews from a couple books that I think you will like. First is a preview of *Up in Smoke*, the first book in the Glock Grannies Cozy Mystery series. Second is a preview of *A Pie to Die For* by Stacey Alabaster - it's part of the popular Bakery Detectives Cozy Mystery series. I really hope you like the samples. If you do, both books are available on Amazon.

- Get Up in Smoke here:
  amazon.com/dp/B06XHKYRRX

- Get A Pie to Die For here:
  amazon.com/dp/B01D6ZVT78

Lastly, if you would like to know about future cozy mysteries by me and the other authors at Fairfield Publishing, make sure to sign up for our Cozy Mystery Newsletter. We will send you our FREE Cozy Mystery Starter Library just for signing up. All the details are on the next page.

FAIRFIELD COZY MYSTERY NEWSLETTER

Make sure you sign up for the Fairfield Cozy Mystery Newsletter so you can keep up with our latest releases. When you sign up, **we will send you our FREE Cozy Mystery Starter Library!**

FairfieldPublishing.com/cozy-newsletter/

After you sign up to get your Free Starter Library, turn the page and check out the poems, recipe, and previews.

Thread

You cling to me like no other,
Across my chest, I see you struggle.
Do not let go, you'll fly away,
Hold me forever, I'm yours to snuggle.

But, alas, you bid me ado,
Your time with me is dead.
I must be such a bore to you,
Fly away little thread.

Unsightly Crack

A crack is a crack

No matter the size.
Most are unsightly
A pain to the eyes.

Some are large
Some never seen.
Some should not be noticed
So pull up your jeans.

My Friend

My little friend
In a bowl you swim
Swish, swish goes his fin
Round and round, swim, swim, swim

You have no name
There is no rush
Fish don't live long
Soon you'll be flushed

GRANDMA GRETA'S FAMOUS SUGAR COOKIE RECIPE

(FROSTING RECIPE BELOW)

INGREDIENTS

1 ½ cups (3 sticks) butter softened to room temperature

1 ½ cups granulated sugar

½ cup powdered sugar

4 large eggs

1 teaspoon vanilla

½ teaspoon almond extract (optional – Grandma Greta doesn't use it, but you can)

½ teaspoon lemon zest (you can use as much as 1 tablespoon if you like lemony cookies)

5 cups all-purpose flour

2 teaspoons baking powder

1 teaspoon salt

DIRECTIONS

1. Preheat oven to 400 degrees.
2. In a large bowl, cream together both sugars and the butter until it's light and fluffy (usually takes about 3-4 minutes).
3. Add the eggs one at a time, mixing each one well before you add another.
4. Add in vanilla, almond extract and lemon zest. Mix.
5. Add baking powder, salt and just two cups of the flour. Once it's mixed well, add the other 3 cups of flour and mix just until all the flour is incorporated and the dough is soft and smooth.

THE DOUGH CAN BE WRAPPED in plastic wrap and in kept in the fridge for up to a week or you can roll it out right away. If you do decide to roll it out right away, it will be a bit too sticky. Add ¼ - ½ cup more flour to remedy this.

GRANDMA GRETA LIKES to do it this way:

Divide the dough into two or four equal parts. Sprinkle a little bit of flour (or powdered sugar) on some parchment paper. Your parchment paper should be large enough to contain the dough once it's rolled out. Grab one of the sections of dough and put it in the middle of the paper. Sprinkle on a little more flour or powdered sugar (it doesn't take much) and put another piece of parchment paper on top. Flatten with your hand and then roll into a ¼ inch thickness (Grandma likes her cookies thick). Once you have it rolled out to your desired thickness, gently peel away the paper so it's not sticking to it and then put the paper back on. Flip it over and do the same to the other side. Now you have a nice section of rolled out dough sandwiched between two pieces of parchment paper. Set aside and do the same to the left-over sections. Once finished, stack and put in the fridge! No mess rolling them out, and they'll be ready for the grandkids. Grandma Greta likes to make sure each kid has their own cookie section to work with.

When ready to use, take out of the fridge and cut out the cookies right on the paper. Roll out left over cookie dough using the same method and keep cutting until you run out of dough.

To cook:

- Put cookies on either a greased cookie sheet or cookie sheet lined with parchment paper (Grandma Greta uses parchment paper).
- Bake for 7-8 minutes. Don't over bake! Don't even let these tasty cookies get a little brown – they should be soft with not even a hint of

brown around the edges. Trust Grandma on this. You'll thank her later. She only bakes hers for 7 minutes.

- Cool completely on a wire rack before frosting.

Frosting Recipe

Ingredients

1 cup butter, softened to room temperature

1 teaspoon pure vanilla extract

4 cups powdered sugar

4-6 tablespoons of heavy cream (Grandma Greta uses 6 because she likes it nice and creamy)

Directions

1. Beat the softened butter and the vanilla extract until the butter is nice and creamy. This take about 3 minutes. Since Grandma's arms get tired she uses her big mixer with the paddle attachment but you can use a handheld mixer if you want. At the end of 3

minutes the butter should be creamy and lighter in color.

2. Gradually add the powdered sugar, scraping the bowl often.

3. Increase the mixer speed to medium-high and add in the heavy cream a little at a time. If you accidentally put in too much milk and it's a little too thin, just add more powdered sugar.

4. Add food coloring if you like. Grandma Greta uses Wilton's gel food coloring.

TIPS FOR COOKIES and frosting

AS TEMPTING AS IT IS, don't soften your butter by putting it in the microwave. If you do and you end up with some melty spots, your frosting won't be as creamy and your cookies will end up being greasy (nobody wants that).

PREVIEW: UP IN SMOKE

I COULD FEEL MY HAIR PUFFING UP LIKE COTTON CANDY in the humidity as I stepped outside the Miami airport. I pushed a sticky strand from my face, and I wished for a minute that it were a cheerful pink instead of dirty blond, just to complete the illusion.

"Thank you so much for picking me up from the

airport." I smiled at the sprightly old lady I was struggling to keep up with. "But why did you say my grandmother couldn't pick me up?"

"I didn't say." She turned and gave me a toothy grin —clearly none of them original—and winked. "I parked over here."

When we got to her car, she opened the trunk and threw in the sign she had been holding when she met me in baggage claim. The letters were done in gold glitter glue and she had drawn flowers with markers all around the edges. My name "Nikki Rae Parker" flashed when the sun reflected off of them, temporarily blinding me.

"I can tell you put a lot of work into that sign." I carefully put my luggage to the side of it, making sure not to touch her sign—partially because I didn't want to crush it and partially because it didn't look like the glue had dried yet.

"Well, your grandmother didn't give me much time to make it. I only had about ten minutes." She glanced at the sign proudly before closing the trunk. She looked me in the eyes. "Let's get on the road. We can chit chat in the car."

With that, she climbed in and clicked on her seat belt. As I got in, she was applying a thick coat of bright red lipstick while looking in the rearview mirror. "Gotta look sharp in case we get pulled over." She winked again, her heavily wrinkled eyelid looking like it thought about staying closed before it sprung back up again.

I thought about her words for a moment. She must get pulled over a lot, I thought. Poor old lady. I could picture her going ten miles an hour while the rest of Miami flew by her.

"Better buckle up." She pinched her lips together before blotting them slightly on a tissue. She smiled at me and for a moment, I was jealous of her pouty lips, every line filled in by layers and layers of red.

I did as I was told and buckled my seat belt before I sunk down into her caramel leather seats. I was exhausted, both physically and mentally, from the trip. I closed my eyes and tried to forget my troubles, taking in a deep breath and letting it out slowly to give all my worry and fear ample time to escape my body. For the first time since I had made the decision to come here, I felt at peace. Unfortunately, it was short-lived.

The sound of squealing tires filled the air and my eyes flung open to see this old lady zigzagging through the parking garage. She took the turns without hitting the brakes, hugging each curve like a racecar driver. When we exited the garage and turned onto the street, she broke out in laughter. "That's my favorite part!"

I tugged my seat belt to make sure it was on tight. This was not going to be the relaxing drive I had thought it would be.

We hit the highway and I felt like I was in an arcade

game. She wove in and out of traffic at a speed I was sure matched her old age.

"Ya know, the older I get the worse other people drive." She took one hand off the wheel and started to rummage through her purse, which sat between us.

"Um, can I help you with something?" My nerves were starting to get the best of me as her eyes were focused more on her purse than the road.

"Oh no, I've got it. I'm sure it's in here somewhere." She dug a little more, pulling out a package of AA batteries and then a ham sandwich.

Brake lights lit up in front of us and I screamed, bracing myself for impact. The old woman glanced up and pulled the car to the left in a quick jerk before returning to her purse. Horns blared from behind us.

"There it is!" She pulled out a package of wintergreen Life Savers. "Do you want one?"

"No, thank you." I could barely get the words out.

"I learned a long time ago that it was easier if I just drove and did my thing instead of worrying about what all the other drivers were doing. It's easier for them to get out of my way instead of me getting out of theirs. My reflexes aren't what they used to be." She popped a mint in her mouth and smiled. "I love wintergreen. I don't know why peppermint is more popular. Peppermint is so stuffy; wintergreen is fun."

She seemed to get in a groove with her driving and soon my grip was loosening on the sides of the seat, the blood slowly returning to my knuckles. Suddenly I realized I hadn't asked her name.

"I was so confused when you picked me up from the airport instead of my Grandma Dean that I never asked your name."

She didn't respond, just kept her eyes on the road with a steely look on her face. I was happy to see her finally being serious about driving, so I turned to look out the window. "It's beautiful here," I said after a few minutes of silence. I turned to look at her again and noticed that she was still focused straight ahead. I stared at her for a moment and realized she never blinked. Panic rose through my chest.

"Ma'am!" I shouted as I leaned forward to take the wheel. "Are you okay?"

She suddenly sprung to action, screaming and jerking the wheel to the left. Her screaming caused me to scream and I grabbed the wheel and pulled it to the right, trying to get us back in our lane. We continued to scream until the car stopped teetering and settled down to a nice hum on the road.

"Are you trying to kill us?" The woman's voice was hoarse and she seemed out of breath.

"I tried to talk to you and you didn't answer!" I practically shouted. "I thought you had a heart attack or something!"

"You almost gave me one!" She flashed me a dirty look. "And you made me swallow my mint. You're lucky I didn't choke to death!"

"I'm sorry." As I said the words, I noticed my heart was beating in my ears. "I really thought something had happened to you."

She was quiet for a moment. "Well, to be honest with you, I did doze off for a moment." She looked at me, pride spreading across her face. "I sleep with my eyes open. Do you know anyone who can do that?"

Before I could answer, she was telling me about her friend Delores who "claimed" she could sleep with her eyes open but, as it turned out, just slept with one eye half-open because she had a stroke and it wouldn't close all the way.

I sat there in silence before saying a quick prayer. My hands resumed their spot around the seat cushion and I could feel the blood draining from my knuckles yet again.

"So what was it you tried to talk to me about before you nearly killed us?"

I swallowed hard, trying to push away the irritation that fought to come out.

"I asked you what your name was." I stared at her and decided right then that I wouldn't take my eyes off of her for the rest of the trip. I would make sure she stayed awake, even if it meant talking to her the entire time.

"Oh yes! My name is Hattie Sue Miller," she said with a bit of arrogance. She glanced at me. "My father used to own most of this land." She motioned to either side of us. "Until he sold it and made a fortune." She gave me a look and dropped her voice to a whisper as she raised one eyebrow. "Of course we don't talk about money. That would be inappropriate." She said that last part like I had just asked her when she had last had sex. I felt ashamed until I realized I had never asked her about her money; I had simply asked her name. This woman was a nut. Didn't Grandma Dean have any other friends she could've sent to get me?

For the next hour or so, I asked her all kinds of questions to keep her awake—none of them about money or anything I thought might lead to money. If what she told me was true, she had a very interesting upbringing. She claimed to be related to Julia Tuttle, the woman who founded Miami. Her stories of how she got a railroad company to agree to build tracks there were fascinating. It wasn't until she told me she was also related to Michael Jackson that I started to question how true her stories were.

"We're almost there! Geraldine will be so happy to see you. You're all she's talked about the last two weeks." She pulled into a street lined with palm trees. "You're going to love it here." She smiled as she drove. "I've lived here a long time. It's far enough away from the city that you don't have all that hullaballoo, but big enough that you can eat at a different restaurant every day for a month."

When we entered the downtown area, heavy gray smoke hung in the air, and the road was blocked by a fire truck and two police cars.

"Oh no! I think there might have been a fire!" I leaned forward in my seat, trying to get a better look.

"Of course there was a fire!" Hattie huffed like I was an idiot. "That's why Geraldine sent me to get you!"

"What?! Is she okay?" I scanned the crowd and saw her immediately. She was easy to spot, even at our distance.

"Oh yes. She's fine. Her shop went up in flames as she was headed out the door. She got the call from a neighboring store owner and called me right away to go get you. Honestly, I barely had time to make you a sign." She acted like Grandma Dean had really put her in a bad position, leaving her only minutes to get my name on a piece of poster board.

Hattie pulled over and I jumped out; I'd come back for my luggage later. As I made my way toward the crowd, I was amazed at how little my Grandma Dean—or Grandma Dean-Dean, as I had called her since I was a little girl—had changed. Her bleach blonde hair was nearly white and cut in a cute bob that was level with her chin. She wore skintight light blue denim capris, which hugged her tiny frame. Her bright white t-shirt was the background for a long colorful necklace that appeared to be a string of beads. Thanks to a pair of bright red heels, she stood eye to eye with the fireman she was talking to.

I ran up to her and called out to her. "Grandma! Are you okay?" She flashed me a look of disgust before she smiled weakly at the fireman and said something I couldn't make out.

She turned her back to him and grabbed me by the arm. "I told you to never call me that!" She softened her tone then looked me over. "You look exhausted! Was it the flight or riding with that crazy Hattie?" She didn't give me time to answer. "Joe, this is my daughter's daughter, Nikki."

Joe smiled. I wasn't sure if it was his perfectly white teeth that got my attention, his uniform or his sparkling blue eyes, but I was immediately speechless. I tried to say hello, but the words stuck in my throat.

"Nikki, this is Joe Dellucci. He was born in New Jersey but his parents came from Italy. Isn't that right, Joe?"

I was disappointed when Joe answered without a New Jersey accent. Grandma Dean continued to tell me about Joe's heritage, which reminded me of Hattie. Apparently once you got to a certain age, you automatically became interested in people's backgrounds.

He must have noticed the look of disappointment on my face. "My family moved here when I was ten. My accent only slips in when I'm tired." His face lit up with a smile, causing mine to do the same. "Or when I eat pizza." I had no idea what he meant by that, but it caused me to break out in nervous laughter. Grandma Dean's look of embarrassment finally snapped me out of it.

"Well, Miss Dean. If I hear anything else, I'll let you know. In the meantime, call your insurance company. I'm sure they'll get you in touch with a good fire restoration service. If not, let me know. My brother's in the business."

He handed her a business card and I saw the name in red letters across the front: *Clean-up Guys.* Not a very catchy name. Then suddenly it hit me. A fireman with a brother who does fire restoration? Seemed a little fishy. Joe must have noticed my expression, because he chimed in. "Our house burned down when I was eight and Alex was twelve. I guess it had an impact on us."

Grandma Dean took the card and put it in her back pocket. "Thanks, Joe. I'll give Alex a call this afternoon."

They said their good-byes and as Joe walked away, Grandma Dean turned toward me. "What did I tell you about calling me 'Grandma' in public?" Her voice was barely over a whisper. "I've given you a list of names that are appropriate and I don't understand why you don't use one of them!"

"I'm not calling you Coco!" My mind tried to think of the other names on the list. Peaches? Was that on there? Whatever it was, they all sounded ridiculous.

"There is nothing wrong with Coco!" She pulled away from me and ran a hand through her hair as a woman approached us.

"Geraldine, I'm so sorry to hear about the fire!" The

SHANNON VANBERGEN

woman hugged Grandma Dean. "Do they know what started it?"

"No, but Joe's on it. He'll figure it out. I'm sure it was wiring or something. You know how these old buildings are."

The woman nodded in agreement. "If you need anything, please let me know." She hugged Grandma again and gave her a look of pity.

"Bev, this is my...daughter's daughter, Nikki."

I rolled my eyes. She couldn't even say granddaughter. I wondered if she would come up with some crazy name to replace that too.

"It's nice to meet you," Bev said without actually looking at me. She looked worried. Her drawn-on eyebrows were pinched together, creating a little bulge between them. "If you hear anything about what started it, please be sure to let me know."

Grandma turned to me as the woman walked away. "She owns the only other antique store on this block. I'm sure she's happy as a clam that her competition is out for a while," Grandma said, almost with a laugh.

I gasped. "Do you think she did it? Do you think she set fire to your shop?"

"Oh, honey, don't go jumping to conclusions like that. She would never hurt a fly." Grandma looked around. "Where's your luggage?"

I turned to point toward Hattie's car, but it was gone.

Grandma let out a loud laugh. "Hattie took off with your luggage? Well, then let's go get it."

Thanks for reading the sample of *Up in Smoke*. I really hope you liked it.

Make sure you turn to the next page for the preview of *A Pie to Die For*.

PREVIEW: A PIE TO DIE FOR

"But you don't understand, I use only the finest, organic ingredients." My voice was high-pitched as I pleaded my case to the policeman. Oh, this was just like an episode of Criminal Point. Hey, I wondered who the killer turned out to be. I shook my head. That's not important, Rachael, I scolded myself. *What's important is getting yourself off this murder charge.* Still, I hoped Pippa had recorded the ending of the episode.

I tried to steady my breathing as Jackson—Detective Whitaker—entered the room and threw a folder on the table, before studying the contents as though he was cramming for a test he had to take the next day. He rubbed his temples and frowned.

Is he even going to make eye contact with me? Is he just going to completely ignore the interaction we had at the fair? Pretend it never even happened.

"Jackson..." I started, before I was met with a steely

glare. "Detective. Surely you can't think I had anything to do with this?"

Jackson looked up at me slowly. "Had you ever had any contact with Mrs. Batters before today?"

I shifted in my seat. "Yes," I had to admit. "I knew her a little from the store. She was always quite antagonistic towards me, but I'd never try to kill her!"

"Witnesses near the scene said that you two had an argument." He gave me that same steely glare. Where was the charming, flirty, sweet guy I'd meet earlier? He was now buried beneath a suit and a huge attitude.

"Well...it wasn't an argument...she was just...winding me up, like she always does."

Jackson shot me a sharp look. "So, she was annoying you? Was she making you angry?"

"Well... Well..." I tripped over my words. He was now making me nervous for an entirely different reason than he had earlier. Those butterflies were back, but now they felt like daggers.

Come on, Rach. Everyone knows that the first suspect in Criminal Point is not the one that actually did it.

But how many people had Jackson already interviewed? Maybe he was saving me for last. Gosh, maybe my cherry pie had actually killed the woman!

"Answer the question please, Miss Robinson."

"Not angry, no. I was just frustrated."

"Frustrated?" A smile curled at his lips before he pounced. "Frustrated with Mrs. Batters?"

"No! The situation. Come on—you were there!" I

SHANNON VANBERGEN

tried to appeal to his sympathies, but he remained a brick wall.

"It doesn't matter whether I was there or not. That is entirely besides the point." He said the words a little too forcefully.

I swallowed. "I couldn't get any customers to try my cakes, and Bakermatic was luring everyone away with their free samples." I stopped as my brows shot up involuntarily. "Jackson! Sorry, Detective. Mrs. Batters ate at Bakermatic as well!"

My words came out in a stream of breathless blabber as I raced to get them out. "Bakermatic must be to blame! They cut corners, they use cheap ingredients. Oh, and I know how much Mrs. Batters loved their food! She was always eating there. Believe me, she made that very clear to me."

Jackson sat back and folded his arms across his chest. "Don't try to solve this case for us."

I sealed my lips. *Looks like I might have to at this rate.*

"We are investigating every place Mrs. Batters ate today. You don't need to worry about that."

I leaned forward and banged my palm on the table. "But I do need to worry about it! This is my job, my livelihood...my life on the line. If people think I am to blame, that will be the final nail in my bakery's coffin!" Oh, what a day. And I'd thought it was bad enough that I hadn't gotten any customers at my stand. Now I was being accused of killing a woman!

I could have sworn I saw a flicker of sympathy

finally crawl across Jackson's face. He stood up and readjusted his tie, but he still refused to make full eye contact. "You're free to go, Miss Robinson," he said gently. There was that tone from earlier, finally. He seemed recognizable as a human at long last.

"Really?"

He nodded. "For the moment. But we might have some more questions for you later, so don't leave town."

I tried to make eye contact with him as I left, squirreling out from underneath his arm as he held the door open for me, but he just kept staring at the floor.

Did that mean he wasn't coming back to my bakery after all?

PIPPA WAS STILL WAITING for me when I returned home later that evening. There was a chill in the air, which meant that I headed straight for a blanket and the fireplace when I finally crawled in through the door. Pippa shot me a sympathetic look as I curled up and crumbled in front of the flames. *How had today gone so wrong, so quickly?*

"I recorded the last part of the show," Pippa said softly. "If you're up for watching it."

I groaned and lay on the carpet, my back straight against the floor like I was a little kid. "I don't think I can stomach it after what I just went through. Can you believe it? Accusing ME of killing Mrs. Batters? When I *know* that Bakermatic is to blame. I mean, Pippa, they must be! But this detective wouldn't even listen to me when I was trying to explain Bakermatic's dodgy practices to him."

Pippa leaned forward and took the lid off a pot, the smell of the brew hitting my nose. "Pippa, what is that?"

She grinned and stirred it, which only made the smell worse. I leaned back and covered my nose. "Thought it might be a bit heavy for you. I basically took every herb, tea, and spice that you had in your cabinet and came up with this! I call it 'Pippa's Delight'!"

"Yeah well, it doesn't sound too delightful." I sat up and scrunched up my nose. "Oh, what the heck—pour me a cup."

"Are you sure?" Pippa asked with a cheeky grin.

"Go on. I'll be brave."

I braced myself as the brown liquid hit the white mug.

It was as disgusting as I had imagined, but at least it made me laugh when the pungent concoction hit my tongue. Pippa always had a way of cheering me up. If it wasn't her unusual concoctions, or her ever changing hair color—red this week but pink the last, and purple a week before that—then it was her never-ending array of careers and job changes that entertained me and kept me on my toes. When you're trying to run your own business, forced to be responsible day in and day out, you have to live vicariously through some of your more free-spirited friends. And Pippa was definitely that: free-spirited.

"Hey!" I said suddenly, as an idea began to brew in my brain. I didn't know if it was the tea that suddenly brought all my senses to life or what it was, but I found myself slamming my mug on the table with new found enthusiasm. "Pippa, have you got a job at the moment?" I could never keep up with Pippa's present state of employment.

She shrugged as she kicked her feet up and lay back on the sofa. "Not really! I mean, I've got a couple of things in the works. Why's that?"

I pondered for a moment. "Pippa, if you could get a job at Bakermatic, you could see first hand what they're up to!" My voice was a rush of excitement as I clapped my hands together. "You would get to find out the ways they cut corners, the bad ingredients they use, and, if you were really lucky, you might even overhear someone say something about Mrs. Batters!"

A gleam appeared in Pippa's green eyes. "Well, I do need a job, especially after today."

I raced on. "Yes! And you've got plenty of experience working in cafes."

"Yeah. I've worked in hundreds of places." She took a sip of the tea and managed to swallow it. She actually seemed to enjoy it.

"I know you've got a lot of experience. You're sure to get the job. They're always looking for part-timers."

Unfortunately, Bakermatic was planning on expanding the storefront even further, and that meant they were looking for even more employees to fill their big yellow store. "Pippa, this is the perfect plan! We'll get you an application first thing in the morning. Then you can start investigating!"

Pippa raised her eyebrows. "Investigating?"

I nodded and lay my head back down on the carpet. "Criminal Point—Belldale Style! Bakery Investigation Unit! I will investigate and do what I can from my end as well! Perhaps I could talk to people from all the other food stalls! Oh, Pippa, we're going to make a crack team of detectives!"

"The Bakery Detectives!"

We both started giggling but, as the full weight of the day's events started to pile up on me, I felt my stomach tighten. It might seem fun to send Pippa in to spy on Bakermatic, but this was serious. My bakery, my livelihood, and even my own freedom depended on it.

THANKS FOR READING a sample of *A Pie to Die For*. I really hope you liked it.

YOU CAN GET it for free by signing up for our newsletter.

FairfieldPublishing.com/cozy-newsletter/